I0693194

TRENCH COAT COUNTRY

A Bradshaw Short Story Collection

A V IAIN

DIII

Contents

CASE NUMBER ONE

1

WATER SPURTED UP from the drinking fountain, spraying into the air and landing on the polished tiles, already forming the beginnings of what was going to be a mighty big puddle. Bradshaw paused at the spillage, looking it over, first from the puddle then to the leaking tap. Bradshaw was stick-thin, well over six foot six and wearing his distinctive all-black outfit, including a wide-brimmed—black, of course—hat which offered only a clear view of his pitted chin, leaving the rest of his face in ambiguous shadow.

Officer Adrian Thompson of the Sesney Police Force—a particularly quiet force, unused to scandal or controversy—sidled up alongside Bradshaw, his eyes also falling onto that same fountain. "Don't worry about that, we'll get that cleaned up. Plumber's on his way."

Bradshaw, however, remained unmoved, continuing to stare at the nascent lake puddling into existence at his mud-clodden, ankle-high boots.

Adrian, for a second or so, looked at little lost—most likely feeling a little apprehensive when, that morning, he'd got the call from the office telling him to run by the bus station and pick up this *Bradshaw* guy. And imagine his surprise when he'd caught sight of this specimen. The man was like a stick insect, just . . . impossibly built. It was a wonder he didn't topple over in a stiff breeze.

Adrian reached up and scratched the back of his neck, a little bit of sweat glistening there, just a touch of pressure making itself felt. As he did so, he flinched as the burnt patch on his finger rubbed up against his skin—he'd most likely get some cream on it next time he got the chance. "We'd better get moving

—they've been waiting all morning." He glanced up the corridor as if his red-faced boss, Rudder—as he was known—might come barrelling down, waggling his finger, cheeks like a hippo's bum cheeks, spittle gathering in the corners of his mouth as he reprimanded him.

Obviously, feeling somewhat more confident, he risked reaching up and laying a hand—*his* hand—on Bradshaw's shoulder. "Come—"

Bradshaw pivoted round, head cocked to one side, although his face was still in shadow the bottom lip of his mouth showed, and that was enough to give away that he was grimacing. Grimacing hard. When he spoke it was through gritted teeth. "Don't you *ever* touch me."

Adrian flinched, his hand seeming to return to him of its own accord, as if it were a spring-loaded measuring tape. He attempted an ill-fated grin, and it turned out to be *so* ill-fated that it merely shrivelled up and died right there on his lips.

Without another word, and certainly without making eye contact with Adrian, Bradshaw shifted off down the hall, walking with that slight limp of the left leg that—now—Adrian was probably glad that he'd never once brought up, in the way of small talk—or in any other way, for that matter—on the car ride over here.

2

VOICES DRIFTED OUT from Meeting Room Three, along the corridor, loud enough so that they were both in Bradshaw and Adrian's earshot. Bradshaw curtailed his trudge with a sudden halt, apparently to Adrian's great surprise, considering the hunching of his shoulders and the widening of his eyes.

Adrian thought to speak. "They're just—"

Bradshaw glared, if anyone who keeps their facial features hidden can really ever be evidenced to glare, and emitted a quiet, almost silent, "*Shh!*"

From inside the meeting room the voices continued unabated. There was the *rustle* of a shirt sleeve being drawn back, that light *tinkle* of a chain-link watchstrap—a watch being consulted. ". . . So when's this guy showing up, eh?"

"Look, he's worth waiting for, that's all I'm saying." There was a brief pause, as if the speaker was considering whether or not to add the following piece of information—almost as if he *might* have a hunch that someone might be listening, standing right outside the door. But if he did have this *hunch* it certainly didn't lead him to get up out of his seat and go over to the door and check. And so he continued, in a more hushed tone this time, "You know what they call this guy?"

"No, what?"

A pause for effect then, "*The Scarecrow.*"

Another pause and then, his conversational partner, apparently unsure what to do with this information, burst out in loud, throaty guffaws of laughter. With some actual thigh slapping involved. Once he got hold of himself, he faced up to his companion, the echoes of laugher, those heavy sucks of air, still tainting his speech. "You make him sound like some sort of . . . I don't know, some sort of super hero."

The first speaker, the more serious one, remained serious. Obviously he *had not* been laughing. "Well that's not too far from the truth," he said. "The stuff I've heard."

"And what *stuff's* this?"

There was a pregnant break, while the first speaker thought this over, no doubt wanting to make his account seem dramatic perhaps in some attempt to boost his claim's creditability. "I heard that there was this one case—horrible case, right—where this old man and lady had been murdered, way out in the country. I mean this wasn't just anything, this was some real psycho deal—blood up the walls, corpses messed with, you know what I'm talking about, right? Didn't even leave the *damn* dog, as if the dog would've told someone."

He drew a breath, a breath that suggested he had once been a smoker, and how he would *quite like* a cigarette right there and then. "Anyway weird part of the case, the line of inquiry the boys were working to on the case it was all about this couples' savings —had pots of gold, cash money, not well-hidden either. The guys found it on their first pass—hidden behind a bunch of books, you know, in that space you get behind them on the bookcase."

"Yeah," the other man said, sounding a little weary already, like he'd heard one too many of these kinds of procedural tales. "I know the one."

"Murderers didn't think to take it. Thing is, how these guys had left the bodies—the damn *horror* of it—you just knew that they were psychopaths."

"And how'd Bradshaw come to bear on this?"

"Well, about second week into it someone—don't quite remember who, maybe the detective in charge of the case—gets handed this card, plain white card that's just been stuck to the front door of the house one day and all it's got on is this scrawled number, barely legible. Nothing else to do, and onto a total loss with the case, detective gives it a ring—only those damn numbers are so scrawled, downright illegible, that he rings up and gets the wrong number, not once but several times."

Again, he took a sharp intake of breath before continuing—as if relaying this story was akin to a marathon run. "*Finally* gets through to the number, asks all the usual question, 'Who is this?' and 'Where'd you get off leaving this number lying about?' And then, just as he's about to hang up, with no response on the other end, this guy tells them to go look in the basement of the house. Detective tells him there isn't a basement in the house. Guy tells him to pull back the carpet in the library, place they found the money behind the books and look there.

"Well, detective keeps the guy on the line, tells him to wait there—because he's not wanting to be made a fool, and maybe he can hand the phone to one of the techno-kids after he's done if this ends up being a prank phone call, have this punk tracked and bring him in for wasting police time. Only the detective goes into the library tugs up that carpet and, low and behold, finds trapdoor. Well, he just gets down on his haunches and prises that things up—or maybe he got one of the grunts to do it, I don't know—anyway, once he gets it open this real pungent odour seeps into the room, I mean I'm talking post-apocalyptic pestilent, putrescent stink. And there's only one thing, being a cop, you're going to think that is."

"A body?" the other man said.

Obviously coming to the end of the story now, although not sounding like relating it had given him as much confidence he had presumably hoped for when he'd started, he let loose a sigh. "Turns out that old couple—bless 'em—they kept the mother load down in the basement. Jewellery, bars of silver, more cash money. And they weren't stupid either. Sure, that guy got his way into their home, but there wasn't much they could do to stop that, what with them being old. What they did do, though, was set up a tripwire in the basement, so that anyone who got down there—maybe while they were on holiday, whatever, would stumble about in the dark, activate the tripwire and send the trapdoor clattering shut right behind them, trapping the burglar inside."

"Genius."

"Not bad, eh?" the man said, the sound of a smile creeping into his voice. "Needless to say the guy'd been in there a good couple of weeks, maybe a month, and so he was good and ripe. The dog walker was the guy. He used to come round and walk that couples' dog, my guess is that one day he just happened to be passing by and see that basement open." He shook his head. "I mean, from what I heard about those bodies it was a *real* amateur deal—sounds to me like the guy just went nuts, the old people struggled or whatever. He was no murderer—no pro, anyway."

The other man steeped into silence, obviously absorbing the details of the case as only a detective can do. And then, all of a sudden, he broke from his pensive daze. "Just one thing."

"Yeah, what's that?"

"The carpet," he said. "Who smoothed the carpet down after the dog walker got trapped inside?"

3

IN THE CORRIDOR, both Bradshaw and Adrian lurked—listening into everything that was said. Bradshaw decided that this was the moment to blow his cover, and he shifted along the final few steps, to the doorway of the meeting room, peering around the doorframe.

The two men nestled inside. Both sat on their own high-backed, plush black leather chair—with really nice sturdy arms—around the walnut-coloured table. One of the men—the one who had told the story—had white-blond hair, fair features, white-rabbit pink eyelids, he almost seemed like he might be an albino, in fact . . . yes, that's just what he was, an albino.

The other man, on the other hand, was dark, tanned, from some place down south. He looked like a man between shaves, and showers. His suit was rumpled and he looked as if he'd spent a night, or two, parked up in his car, asleep on some hard shoulder somewhere.

Both of the men, understandably considering the delicate point at which their conversation had broken off, exchanged nervous glances, before turning their attention to Bradshaw, who merely towered over them, standing only a couple of paces inside the meeting room door.

Adrian, for some reason, despite quite clearly being the most inferior in the room—the most obviously *not* in charge—decided to spark up and break the ice. "This here's him, detectives, just brought him right now." He shifted his weight from one foot to the other—no doubt finding himself racked with shards of nerves in his belly. "Anyone for a cup of coffee?" he said.

However, both detectives continued to focus on Bradshaw,

both of them apparently caught in a daze—unable to quite believe who it was that was before them. Then the darker detective broke into an uneasy, yellow-teethed smile. The smile was *so* yellow-teethed it looked like his enamel might be growing fur.

He lurched up and out of his seat so quickly that it seemed to be a mere after thought. He crossed the room and extended his hand to Bradshaw. "So pleased to meet you—I've just been hearing all about you from Detective Pinko over here."

Bradshaw examined the hand, as if it were a hunk of mould he'd just discovered in the deeper recesses of his fridge, and then he shook uneasily.

The albino detective rose from his seat. He, too, was smiling, but not in any convincing kind of a way. "That's not my real name," he said. "Pinko's not my real name. Smith, that's my surname—Detective Andrew Smith."

Bradshaw merely grunted by way of reply.

A fraught silence caned the room into submission. Only the gentle *buzz* of the air conditioning, the slight chatter of a conversation between two mothers—passing by with their children outside—broke through.

Both detectives continued to grin away furiously.

The darker detective said, "And I'm Harold. Harold Peterson —Detective Peterson, actually. But you can call me Harold."

This was greeted by another grunt from Bradshaw.

It was Pinko—Smith—who summoned the courage to cut to the chase. "Thing is we've got a case that we need you for—I managed to get your card off one of my colleagues, another detective who you, um, collaborated with on a case a while back." He was sweating now, his eyes becoming more piggy-like. "Well," he said, glancing over to Detective Peterson, "why don't we just take a ride, eh? Probably best way of doing it, no?"

Again, silence draped over the room like a damp cloth, and, again, with a callow tinge, it was Officer Thompson—Adrian who spoke up. "So shall I get the coffee to go?"

4

THEY TOOK TWO CARS to the scene of the murder. Detectives Peterson and Pink . . . Smith travelled together, while Officer Thompson got stuck with Bradshaw, although he wouldn't have made any noises about his obvious dismay if his life would've depended on it—which, if it had come down to it, it probably would have. Needless to say, Detectives Peterson and Smith had a sporty, unmarked car, while Officer Thompson got stuck with a—very much—marked car, complete with flashing lights which were turned off. For now.

Detective Peterson drove the Pinko-Peterson car and it became apparent, quite quickly, that he was recklessly fast driver. He was one of those drivers who goes out of their way to drive offensively—or to put it another way, takes joy in pissing other road users off. From within the Thompson-Bradshaw vehicle, looking through the back window of the Pink-Peterson, a twitch could be observed in Peterson's eye—a leap of delight as he cut someone off, tailgated some hapless lady with kids in the back, on one occasion with one of those: *Baby on-Board* notices, or honked his horn at some lorry driver—no doubt eight or so hours into his shift—and went through that whole police power trip of getting them to pull over for him to pass.

Bradshaw noted all of this with quiet eyes and a discerning grip on the door handle, as Thompson struggled to keep up with Peterson's manic drive, to shape the car through the slight gaps in traffic or to jab his right foot down on that accelerator as the lights turned from wholesome green to stop-right-now red.

As they shot through yet another near miss with a lorry, being rewarded for their reckless driving with a flat and long *honk*, Bradshaw pointed to the steering wheel, which Thompson clutched to for dear life. "What happened to your finger?" he said.

"Oh," Thompson said, not taking his eyes off the road for even a second, "funniest thing, like I was making toast this morning, running a little late, and wouldn't you just know it? Stuck my finger right in there to get it out, and well . . ." He smiled and shrugged, then turned his attention back to the road. "You know how it is."

Bradshaw grunted.

Soon enough they escaped the madness of the dual carriageway and continued on through a rural countryside road, which just about had enough room for two cars to slip by each other. Thompson's wing mirror brushed the grassy verge beside them more than once. And, *finally*, they arrived.

Bradshaw didn't wait for the car to come to a halt before shucking his seatbelt and opening up the passenger door. He paid no attention to the frantic sidelong glance Thompson shot him— the look that can only be managed by someone with some stake in how the car is going to turn out when it's returned to the carpool in the evening.

Bradshaw landed with a gentle dual *thud*, as the soles of his boots came into contact with asphalt. Right away there was a freshness about the place—that whole *countryside* stench. The house sat pretty much alone off the countryside road. It looked a standard two bedroom affair, tight and tidy. Despite what was a muggy day, what with that heavy band of cloud hanging over the whole drive, like a lingering spectre, there was now a chill in the air—a breeze that suggested rain wasn't all that far off. It tasted of rain—rain and blood.

He stood at the garden gate—wooden, splintered around the edges—he ran his fingers around the sides, feeling that familiar, rough, split surface. It smelled too. Of blood.

As he shoved the gate back, listening to it clatter against the similarly-wooden garden fence, he heard the flapping of wings followed by the distinctive *ka-caw* of a crow taking flight, lolloping overhead, then slipping from sight as it passed beyond the trees which stood at the back of the house.

Detectives Peterson and Smith padded up alongside Bradshaw, standing at his shoulder, peering out and trying to take in what it was he was taking in—Smith more so given his greater reverence for the man, what with that story involving the old folks and the dog walker. Then Thompson, of course, joined them last. He'd most likely quickly run a rag over the marked car, taking care to get rid of any fly corpses that might've got stuck there on the drive over.

It was Smith who spoke, looking to fill Bradshaw in. "Right," he said, "so just to give you an—"

Bradshaw, with the grace that only mercurial talent—or *assumed* mercurial talent—can bring, held up his index finger as if testing to see which direction the wind blew in from. However, with Smith, it had the effect of sharply and efficiently buttoning his lip. And then he closed his eyes—at least that could be assumed to be happening in the shadow beneath the rim of his hat—and breathed in deep, his shoulders rising and falling as he did so.

Behind his back, there was a whole load of glance-exchanging going on: Peterson to Smith, Smith to Thompson, and then back round again. And the worst part of it was that Bradshaw just seemed to sense what was going on—like that brainy kid picked upon at school so many times that he does not simply suppose that someone is speaking behind his back but *knows* it.

Bradshaw jerked around irritably, looked all three men up

and down and then said, with pursed lips, "What happened with that fountain, back at the station?"

More exchanging of glances, along with that stunned brain freeze that sets in when someone, who has just been this sort of lurking, ominous presence—has hardly said *anything*—finally says *something*. It was young, naïve Adrian Thompson who spoke up, most likely because he had the closest thing to a rapport with Bradshaw, what with that fragment of conversation back in the car. "I . . . I don't know," Thompson said. "It was like that when I got to the station this morning."

Bradshaw tilted his gaze in the direction of Smith and Peterson, and then, seeing that it was Pinko Smith who squirmed, focussed in on him.

Detective Smith might well have been a good detective, but it appeared that he had a long way to go in terms of his poker face —he would've made a terrible lawyer and be forever doomed to playing the *good* cop. And under that oppressive, dark gaze—that faint lingering smell of halitosis on the air, that lingering murder scene just standing off, shadowing them all, he managed to spit out what it was he was hiding away. But not without a shifty gaze off to Detective Peterson first, as if he were asking permission. "Well, we had a pretty rough time of it this morning . . . you know how it is, what with this case. A lot on the line for the two of us, if you'll allow me to speak frankly."

Officer Thompson flushed a little at this remark, as if he were embarrassed to be overhearing these remarks from superiors. But it was just what Bradshaw brought out in them, made them dish out things that otherwise would've remained in the dark.

Detective Smith continued, "Anyway, we got in there—into the station—first up and all, and, I don't know, we were just having a chat and then Harold here"—he shot him a sidelong glance

—"well, he just about opened up with another of those *Pinko* remarks and I'd just had my fill, you know how it is, someone says something to you and it just catches you on the wrong foot. So, I don't know." He shrugged. "I just snatched up a fire extinguisher, tore it clean off the wall, and had it out with the water fountain."

Bradshaw inclined his head in Peterson's direction as if wanting to have this confirmed by a second source.

Peterson nodded dolefully, breaking off his gaze with Bradshaw—if they'd ever actually been exchanging gazes in the first place, at least Peterson would never know. "That's right," Peterson said. "Just like it happened."

It seemed that at this juncture it would've been natural for Bradshaw to make some vague *hmm* noise or at the very least one of his—growing-to-be-trademark—*groans*. However, he remained totally silent apparently not reacting to this confirmation in any way whatsoever.

Smith, now red-faced over this revelation, glanced back at the house, then jerked his thumb in its direction. "How about we take a look at the scene, eh?"

Once again, Bradshaw failed to respond.

5

THE HOUSE HAD that horribly lingering stench of bleach—as if someone who'd been frankly appalled at whatever had taken place here had decided to take some measure to distract from whatever terrors lay so far unmasked. Of course that hot, drying taste was there also, accompanying the bleach—drying out even the most salivated tongue. The light, too, despite the large amount of windows, was withery and grey, setting the place in a kind of twilight gloom.

When Bradshaw rounded the doorframe, entering the house, he felt the *snag* of his coat against a loose-hanging nail, which led him to glare at said nail with such ferocity and menacing*ness*, that it was a wonder that it didn't just drop right out of the wall, fall to the ground and burrow its way down to hell of its own volition. But it didn't. Some nails didn't know what was good for them.

Everyone, except Bradshaw, held their shirt or coat collars up to cover their respiratory passages. This had the effect of muffling everyone's words as they spoke and meant dampened groans accompanied by violent arm gestures were the order of the day.

Bradshaw, at least, didn't seem to have much problem with the state of affairs. But then again he seemed not to have much interest in speech at all—his own or otherwise.

They carried on through the house and into, what appeared to be, judging from the shape of the objects covered by sheets, the sitting room. A pair of armchairs, a TV and a settee, which completed the set.

Bradshaw sniffled slightly, and this brought on a twitchy reaction from the other three men, who glanced around to see what it was he was about to say. However, they ended up disappointing as he brought out an off-white handkerchief from one of the inside pockets of his coat and gave his nose a—near silent—blow, before replacing the handkerchief whence it came.

It was Peterson who spread his arms to indicate the room, chancing removing his makeshift nose and mouth cover to speak. "Well," he said, "this is the place." He looked Bradshaw over, but not for long—just like no one *could* look at him for long. He pointed to an area which was covered with a tarpaulin just over in the corner of the sitting room. "That's it, that's where they found the weapon." He inclined his eyebrow in Bradshaw's direction as if hoping this might prompt him to slip out of his muteness. No luck, so he went on. "A damn coat hanger sticking out of the electrical socket, can you believe that?"

Nothing from Bradshaw.

"Yeah," Peterson continued, as if Bradshaw *had* replied, "should've seen the body—I mean, wow, it was like . . . I don't know, what do you think, Pinko? Like a barbeque?"

Pinko—Smith—nodded vigorously and then gazed down at that patch of tarpaulin ostensibly reassembling the image that the two stumbled upon in the first place.

Peterson sighed. "Forensics found all sorts of DNA that wasn't related to the victim on the clothes hanger—only thing they could say was that it was from one person. So we're just looking for one guy, and I think . . ."

But Peterson's words slipped away as he realised that, at this point, for some reason unknown, Bradshaw was gazing upward, seeming to take in the entire room, almost as if he was focussedly *not* trying to look at the tarpaulin, where the victim had been found. No man in the room saw fit to interrupt whatever it was that Bradshaw was sniffing out here.

In the end they just stood there for maybe ten minutes, totally steeped in silence, everyone trying not to make eye contact with anyone else—but most of all the three police trying not to make eye contact with Bradshaw.

And then, as if through nothing at all, as if a mist that had settled in over the scene had finally cleared, Bradshaw raised his head, looked about him—or at least appeared to, because the wide-brimmed hat still covered most of his face—and then, without a word, he headed for the door.

His footsteps sounded chunky on the slatted wooden hallway floors, echoing about him. That bleachy smell had now been tainted with the scent of fresh air—the scent of the leaves and the trees, and the cow manure a couple of fields over, threatening to take the edge of the bleach entirely. And taste buds were refinding their bearings, getting a sense of their surroundings once again, able to be trusted.

Bradshaw arrived outside the house, standing on the front doorstep. He tilted his head back, almost as if he were sniffing the air, like a wolf . . . no, just like that nickname they had for him: The Scarecrow, that was it. It was something about the way that he was so still, so thin, so *unmoveable*. And in that way he seemed constantly pensive, and the gazing upward certainly only added weight to that image.

When he brought his head back down, and looked about him —saw those beleaguered three all standing inside the hallway of the house, just waiting to see what was going to happen, what he was going to say next. But they were to be disappointed, because Bradshaw just shifted on down, off along the path, back toward the cars. And, without asking permission or telling anyone so much as what he had in mind, he opened up the passenger door of the marked car and got inside, even going to the trouble of hitching his seatbelt over his wiry frame and clasping it shut with a satisfying *click*.

For what seemed the umpteenth time that morning, all three

police exchanged glances—one with the other, slowly—and then Peterson let out a long-held sigh, puffing out his cheeks as he did so, giving out again that lingering stench of stale coffee, and that waft of BO that seemed to accompany each of his words. "Guess we're headed back to the station, then."

6

BRADSHAW GAVE no indication that the police station wasn't where they were headed, and so that was where they went. Thompson didn't even flirt with the idea of making conversation this time around, and the case had all the markings of reaching the stages of finality—all that awaited now was Bradshaw's masterstroke, his killing touch. But what would it be, where would it come from?

They trod through the halls, following on Bradshaw's heels, as he apparently made his way back to the meeting room. On the way there, Bradshaw took in the fountain again, which had since been fixed. He lurked over it a moment, gazed down at it, and then moved onward.

However, Bradshaw didn't stop at the meeting room at all. In fact, he continued on his way, going on along the hallway, entering the lockup area of the station—the holding pen. It was sparsely populated today: a shoplifter, a couple of suspected muggers and one kid—not much over eighteen—who had had the nerve to flick a policeman the finger that morning, and was just getting a just dose of what happened when you crossed that Thin Blue Line. Judging from the gentle scent of urine in the air, that metallic taste in the mouth and throat, it was doing the trick all right.

Bradshaw walked them past the holding pen and through to another prison cell—a single cell, meant for the *at risk* or prisoners who put *others* at risk. The baffled officer manning the gate simply buzzed him in, perhaps taking Bradshaw to be a particularly understanding arrest they'd just brought in, and what with those three policemen on his tail he wasn't going to get up to much in the station.

Bradshaw pressed his hand against the cold steel door and pushed his way through into the cell, the first in the row, appropriately marked Cell One. There was a bed which hung down from the wall on less-than-sturdy looking chain links, with a wafer-thin mattress plonked on top, and tiny—*tiny*—rectangular window, no larger than a letterbox set in the wall. The only other furniture was the extremely cold-looking steel toilet . . . but the less said about that the better—although it might be worth adding that the water in the toilet was a particular shade of chemical blue given that the cleaning lady had recently decided to disinfect the thing.

Bradshaw stood with his back to the officers, apparently looking out through the window, through which could only be seen the cold grey, overcast sky.

There were shuffles of impatience from the three men, until it was Peterson who sucked up the courage to prompt Bradshaw for some answers. "So," he said. "Got any fresh ideas?"

Nothing from Bradshaw.

"I mean, what're we doing being led all mysteriously out here —to this prison cell?"

Again, Bradshaw remained totally silent.

"Well? Come on, man, out with it. You've come with this reputation—and all that entails, why don't you tell me what conclusions you've come to, if any?" He sighed then checked over Smith and Thompson. He coloured slightly, the lack of sleep—and surplus of coffee—clearly biting him now. "Look here, if you waste any more of my time then I'm going to have you arrested for wasting police time, do you hear that?"

Still nothing from Bradshaw.

Peterson, apparently not getting any help at all from either Smith or Thompson, took it upon himself to round 'The Scarecrow' and to attempt to peer up into his face. But, of course, all he could see was that shadow. Perhaps a little of Bradshaw's upper lip. And then, apparently getting himself caught up in a bout of rage, he seized hold of Bradshaw's shoulders, digging his fingers into the man's flesh and shook him. At first it was gentle, just a light shake, and then it graduated, got stronger and stronger, until it became clear that Bradshaw had had enough—clear because Bradshaw merely reached out and, with untold strength, gripped both Peterson's forearms with his own dinner plate-sized hands. When Bradshaw spoke it was through gritted teeth, with warm breath and a rough touch.

"You're looking at the killer, right there."

Peterson's lips parted and his eyes appeared to bulge from their sockets. He just about summoned the strength to form the word. ". . . What?"

But it seemed that Bradshaw was not at liberty to explain any further than that, and he merely stepped to one side and then turned to look at Smith and Thompson. He waited with infinite patience, as he had through the entire process.

Peterson now moved his gaze to Thompson and Smith, who remained unmoved—no emotion showed on their faces, only, perhaps, determination, but so slight as almost to go totally unnoticed. "What's he talking about?" Peterson said.

Still, Thompson and Smith stayed quiet.

And then, with all the decorum of a thunderstorm, Bradshaw blew out a sigh, gazed over Thompson and Smith before taking it upon himself to explain. "They did it," he said, as if setting it out in such clear terms might get Peterson's foot on the rung as far as understanding was concerned. "And they did it for attention."

"What?" Peterson said, now unsure whether to look, to his colleagues or to this towering oddball dressed in black.

"It's happened before—just never with police, but I thought it would happen, sooner or later."

Peterson shook his head. "I don't understand at all."

"Detective Smith here, he got my card following that murder case—the one with the dog walker—and it's obvious that he was pretty much tied up in whatever it was . . . whoever it is I am. Problem is, what with Sesney being a pretty small town—small enough not to see murder too often, anyway, or at least *complicated* murders—there wasn't going to be much opportunity. And so they did what they had to do."

"And what's that?"

"They made the murder for themselves."

Peterson all of a sudden seemed to grasp hold of himself. A new steel entered his gaze as these revelations dawned on him and he clenched his fists down by his sides—almost like a cartoon version of a wronged man. "But . . . but," he said, examining Smith, "we were working the case together, how did you—?"

Smith remained stone-faced. "Because *I* didn't commit the murder—nothing to do with *me*. Not the killing part anyway."

And then Peterson's gaze fell on Thompson, and then down to Thompson's hand, in particular the burnt finger. He looked back up. "You did this—with the coat hanger. That was you. You got the burn mark from the electric shock."

Thompson remained just as stone-faced as Smith and then, almost imperceptibly, nodded.

Peterson turned to look at the floor, his eyeballs bobbing about like Ping-Pong balls, putting all the pieces together—tying up all the knots in the case. Next he turned on Smith. "The water fountain, this morning, *that* was you, but . . . ah, I think I see now, you were . . . *angry*."

Finally, Smith did speak up. "It was fraught this morning—I knew it was the end, that there was no turning back. But, I thought, at least, that I'd get to see the great"—he smirked a touch—"*Bradshaw* in action. Finally have something happen in my life." He slipped Thompson a sidelong glance. "And the kid, he was just as keen, wanted to know just as much about him as I did. And so we did it."

All at once the room seemed to snap to attention. The rusty smell of metal, that pungent smell of bleach coming from the toilet and Bradshaw's heavy breathing became too much to bear. And then Peterson responded, cracked right through the tension pulsating all around. He barrelled out of the room, past Thompson and Smith, out into the corridor, and out into the holding area. Hurriedly, not making a lot of sense, he instructed the officer guarding the holding cells to lock down Cell One. And then, right at the last, he remembered Bradshaw, and, feeling nimble footed, no doubt strung out with a combination of sleep-lessness, rage and caffeine, he rushed back inside.

He peered in through the reinforced window of the cell, examining both Smith and Thompson nestled inside. They stared back at him, their gazes empty, resigned. He bent his neck back trying to catch sight of Bradshaw, to see him in there somewhere.

But he wasn't there.

7

ABOUT TWO WEEKS LATER, outside a bus station in the town of Hailsbury, a man wearing a wide-brimmed hat and dressed in all black trod his way through the exhaust fumes, breathing them in just as easily as a fish gulps water. As the bus brakes screeched out through the air, sending some travellers flinching and others, more afflicted, to clutching their ears with their bare hands, the man in black just strode on. Because he was certain of where he was headed.

A man—a *police*man—to be more exact, awaited him, leaning up against his marked car, sipping on a coffee which steamed up in the early morning, chilly air, warming his hands, sending micro jerks of comfort up his spine. And one thing was for certain, that while he absorbed the sight of the man in black there, towering over him, that bitter taste—those final coffee grains at the base of the cup—found their way onto the back of his tongue.

And they were bitter as all hell.

TAKING CARE OF THE NEIGHBOURS

1

I T WAS HAPPENING AGAIN. Cain was sure of it. That steady *thud* of the closing door, those sure heavy footsteps on the floorboards overhead and—he was sure he could hear it—a very slight, but long-held sigh. Barry Tonsworth, his troublesome neighbour, had arrived home from work.

Cain tried to tune himself out most nights because, for goodness' sake, he could do with a little quiet time when he spent the whole day on the phone with clients chirping away in his ear, like so many canaries, wanting to know about the status of their returns, if he'd got their six-page emails or if he could, just maybe, think about giving them a discount on their next consultation. But it was impossible, what with that couple upstairs, Barry's booming baritone voice, and Shirley—his wife's— shrieking responses. And it was every night, without fail. He could've set his damn watch by it.

As he listened to a ticking of the clock he dimly noted his hearing fading from him, Barry's gruff voice, that ever-so-sweet greeting from Shirley, and he knew that once the dust settled, in a matter of moments, it would descend into the age-old melodrama of husband versus wife.

Not tonight, though. Tonight things would be different. Tonight he would get eight hours sleep without interruptions. Tonight he would put a stop to it himself.

He shook off his rubber gloves and set the final plate down with a *clunk* in the drying rack. He gave the calendar a cursory glance, although he knew he had nothing planned for tonight. Tonight would be perfect. Next he made his way across the kitchen, strode right through the sitting room, the TV screen merely a flickering light out of the corner of his eye. He turned the key in the back door. It took him several jiggles as he did battle with the rusted mechanism. With a final jerk he managed to get the damn thing open and he shoulder barged the door open, listening to it creak out on its hinges before clattering up against the brick wall outside.

Cain paused and strained his hearing, trying to work out whether or not Barry and Shirley Tonsworth had heard the slight commotion. But of course they hadn't. He stood there, feeling his musky-smelling work shirt rise and fall against his chest as he breathed. They were still on Phase One—the loved-up greetings, the baby-talk voices, those smoochy kisses that seemed to suck at Cain's skin like leaches.

The night air was fresh and he drank it in, opening his mouth wide to breathe it inside, to freshen his hot-tasting mouth and tongue. Then he proceeded out to the ramshackle shed, nailed together out of several cast-off planks of wood, with a door that just about had enough life left in it to support the buckle holding the padlock. He slipped a smaller key into the padlock and yanked it off, holding it down by his side.

He shot a glance off over his shoulder, back up to the floor above—to the Tonsworths' flat. Tonight he would have vengeance, of that no one would have any doubt whatsoever. This would be the last time he, or anyone else for that matter, had to suffer the Tonsworths' arguments.

Inside the shed it was gloomy, so it was a good thing Cain knew exactly what he had inside, knew his way about its interior in the dark. When he found what he was looking for, he crouched down and smiled for the longest time. After a while he thought he might be pressing wrinkles into his cheeks so he stopped. His fresh-faced appearance was important—that was why clients trusted him with their most intimate financial details. In any case now was the time to be serious.

Deadly serious.

He reached out and slipped the large-bladed knife off its hook. He felt its steady weight in his hand. This would do the trick.

2

BRADSHAW SNIFFED TO HIMSELF as he sat propped
up against the sun-faded green plastic seat in the bus shelter. Exhaust fumes billowed out from the bus he'd just disembarked. It pulled out of the bay with a hiss of hydraulics and then rumbled off up the road. He watched it pull around the corner and then slip from sight.

Bradshaw sniffed again. He was feeling a cold coming on. He had that dry feeling in his throat, the phlegmy taste on his tongue and the tingle in his lungs. He drew his leather trench coat around himself, folding his arms to keep it tight about his chest, to give himself a modicum of warmth. They'd said they'd be here to meet him off the bus. Just went to show you never could trust a cop. Especially when it came to keeping time.

The bright morning sun peeped out from behind a muddy cloud. It seemed strangely out of context, what with the scent of rain in the air, that ominous humidity all pointing to a storm brewing. It was like the sun's pre-emptive, but ultimately futile, strike on what was to be a severely dour day.

He tipped his wide-brimmed hat down over his eyes, to shield himself from the sun rays, and to attempt to fend off the stewing migraine. As he sat there, feeling himself growing a little nauseous what with all his cold symptoms, he heard a light *hum* of an engine, too quiet to be a bus, and he knew instantly—just from its pitch—that it was a police car, that estate two-litre model. Without the white paint and fluorescent strips, the lights perched on its roof, the car would've looked just like a family car —perhaps a dad driving his kids to the zoo.

The car rumbled up to the pavement and stopped beside him. The engine idled and he listened to the window wind down with that electric whine. Bradshaw, still wary of the sun beating down on him from up above, glanced out from beneath the brim of his hat.

A peach-cheeked officer peered out through the driver's window. He had a broad grin fixed on his face and naïve, sea-blue eyes. Bradshaw was even convinced, just for a moment, that he caught a whiff of baby powder wafting out from the car. Did these police officers get younger every year or was he just getting older?

Feeling the plastic seat creaking beneath his shifting weight, Bradshaw glanced deeper into the car and took in the other officer. Younger, if anything. Although the car was steeped in shadow, he could make out the smoothed-down, possibly gelled, black hair and the delicate cherub-like features. It looked like his mother had dabbed some rouge on his cheeks just before she tucked the tail of his shirt into the back of his trousers and kissed him on the forehead on his way out the door to work.

Bradshaw's cold symptoms worsened. He felt his sinuses getting more and more blocked. He had to sniff more just to keep the air flowing through his nostrils and into his lungs. Every breath was a struggle.

"Bradshaw?" Peach Cheeks said.

Bradshaw cleared his throat then, reluctantly, pushed himself up from the plastic seat. Even though he felt like crap he had a moment to enjoy that look he got when he stood up to full height, those widened eyes, those slightly parted lips, the way people leaned a little back from him. Last time he'd measured he'd stood at just a hair over six foot six. He had a way of sitting, slightly hunched over, that made people think he was more likely six, six one at most. Until he stood up.

Cherub Features leaned over his partner, and looked out the window too. He whistled long and hard, piercing in a way that made Bradshaw's migraine pound away at his temples. "My, mister, you're pretty big, aintcha?"

Bradshaw looked over the car, to the two boys . . . police officers, and then, without a word to either, he unhooked the back door handle and stepped inside. He slumped onto the back seat and brought the door closed behind him with a smart *thump*.

He looked at the backs of the heads of the policemen, Peach Cheeks with his blond hair, sitting in the driver's seat, and Cherub Features, black-haired, in the passenger seat. They were behind the wire mesh, of course. And Bradshaw was all too aware that now he had shut the door behind him he would have no way of escaping from the car without either of these fresh-faced police's say-so. Good thing they had no reason to hold him. Nothing they could prove anyway.

Peach Cheeks and Cherub Features muttered something between them. Peach Cheeks glanced over his shoulder, looked to Bradshaw, smiled weakly, then turned his attention back to the controls of the car.

Cherub Features wasn't so brave. His earlier cocksureness had suddenly faded, as it always seemed to with young cops. Bradshaw only noticed him regarding him through the relative safety of the wing mirror. It only took Bradshaw one menacing glare to put a stop to that minor act of voyeurism.

As they puttered through the morning traffic, Peach Cheeks driving like a kid who'd just passed his test—and for all Bradshaw knew he just had. Bradshaw squirmed on the backseat, never able to get comfortable with that rough-weave fabric rustling up against his leather jacket with each movement of the car. He much preferred to travel by bus. Less tossing around. You didn't feel every last bump in a bus.

About twenty minutes later they pulled up outside a house. Bradshaw stared out at it from under glass. It was a simple two-floor house that had been converted into a pair of flats, or so he could tell from the stairway leading up around the outside. He had always wondered how people could live like this. In houses.

Trapped here in the backseat of the car, that smell of baby powder, or whatever the hell it was, was starting to get on his nerves, settling on his tongue, getting caught at the back of his throat like dust. He cleared his throat several times but no matter how many times he did he couldn't shake the sensation.

Peach Cheeks, who was blazing an early case for being the brave one of this duo, glanced back over his shoulder, through that mesh, and said, "Want me to get you a glass of water?"

Bradshaw grunted, then nodded to the back door.

Peach Cheeks flashed his eyebrows. "Oh, right, almost forgot," he said, hauling himself out of his seat and padding round the car to the back door.

In the time it took Peach Cheeks to get round to the back door, Bradshaw noted the slightly uncomfortable silence brewing between himself and Cherub Features. Bradshaw took the opportunity to have another go at clearing his throat. He still couldn't loosen that sour taste of baby powder but he was quite satisfied to see Cherub Features flinch in his seat, and keep up that thousand-yard stare out through the windscreen.

A single yellow and black ribbon surrounded the perimeter of the crime scene. Another officer stood by the tape. He briefly challenged Bradshaw, but whether it was Bradshaw's height, his mighty halitosis, or just that muttered explanation from Peach Cheeks, the officer let them through.

Bradshaw's heels thudded up the cement stairs which led up to the upper floor of the house, where the murder had taken place. He felt both Peach Cheeks and Cherub Features on his heels the whole time and he got that unsettling feeling that they were watching and waiting for him to do something spectacular.

Perhaps if they looked close—real close—they might just see something.

Dried blood stank out the flat. That slightly tangy, rusty smell. Even despite his brewing cold, Bradshaw could smell that. He glanced about the flat, to the bodies. Three of them. Two men. One woman. Bradshaw cocked the rim of his hat back to get a better look, but not so far back that anyone might be able to look him in the eye. A hatchet job, that was what this had been. Only a matter of seconds later did Bradshaw noticed the suited man standing beside him, wide-eyed, looking like he was bursting at the seams to speak with him. Bradshaw turned his gaze in his direction, giving him permission to speak.

The suited man wore a tortoise-shell brown suit with a cream shirt beneath. He had a rose-coloured tie knotted about his neck. He looked like he'd bought the suit about three or four years ago, when he'd had two or three inches less on the waist. His neck fat bulged out around the collar of his shirt. Bradshaw, himself trim, always looked down on those, around the same age as him—late forties, early fifties—who let themselves go in such a way. *Let it all hang out*, as the kids in his day would've said.

The suited man thrust his hand at Bradshaw. "Detective Horowitz. Glad to meet you. Bradshaw, isn't it? I have to say I've heard a great deal about you."

Bradshaw regarded the hand a second, then accepted it, squeezing lightly and feeling the man's light perspiration there. He thought he could smell that sour sweat on him, almost taste its saltiness on his tongue. He retrieved his hand and tucked it back into the pocket of his leather jacket, a mirror image of the other hand.

Detective Horowitz glanced over Peach Cheeks and Cherub Features with a slight raise of the eyebrows, as if he suspected this might be some sort of a wind up, whether this towering specimen before them, this razor-thin man was for real. He looked back to Bradshaw, apparently satisfied to accept things as they were. "Right, Mr Bradshaw, over here, come and take a closer look."

Bradshaw stared across to the kitchenette installed at the street-side of the flat, almost tucked out of the way like an after thought. There was a stove, with burnt-on sauces of various types, and then there was a much splattered microwave. What caught his attention, however, was the wide-open window, its latch, he saw, had been broken off and the sad hump of twisted metal lay on the kitchen counter with a small plastic placard with a red number three propped up beside it.

"Mr Bradshaw?"

Bradshaw turned back to the matter at hand, to Horowitz who was now lurking back from the bodies. His complexion looked to have paled a little. Bradshaw couldn't blame him. Not really. This was a nasty job.

Bradshaw stood over the bodies, hands still stuffed into the pockets of his leather jacket. He looked to the woman first. She wore a pair of jeans and a pink strappy top. She wore a single shoe—a heeled leather boot—the other of which, he saw looking a metre or so to the left, lay on its side. It had come off in the struggle. He caught the faint scent of her perfume. It reminded him of pine needles. Just like almost all the cop cars smelled like. Except for Peach Cheeks, that was. He guessed they got those little pine tree fresheners on some kind of wholesale deal.

A knot formed in Bradshaw's throat and he coughed it out of place, swallowed the steely-tasting phlegm down and then took in the first man. He was wearing a wife-beater vest, tufts of wiry black hair showed through the thin white shirt. Bradshaw had always resented hairy men, in a way. He wondered if it went back to school, when he had echoes of some long-repressed memory, of some bully or other, comparing his hairlessness to a baby rat's ball sack.

The other man was still dressed in, what he supposed to be, his work suit—a pale grey affair, with a tie a shade or two of grey darker. Bradshaw supposed he'd got some fashion consultant on the case there. Everything about the man screamed accountant, right down to those cross-hatch design socks, those slight blobs of red and yellow there, a kind of rebellion against the otherwise straight suit.

"So?" Horowitz said. "Got anything?"

Bradshaw gave him a stiff glare, then looked back over the bodies. It went without saying that they were all covered in blood. In fact, it went without saying that the whole damn flat was covered in blood. If Bradshaw had been forced to reconstruct the scene he might've had them all dashing about, bleeding freely, before all toppling over into this, rather organised, heap. But no. He suspected something far more complex here. If it hadn't been complex the police never would've called him in in the first place.

Horowitz followed Bradshaw's gaze, or clearly thought he did. "Guy's name's Cain Thompson, lives in the place downstairs. He was an—"

"Accountant," Bradshaw said. "Yes, I know."

Horowitz seemed startled a moment, but soon got over it. He cleared his throat and looked about him as if he might be shown up to be some sort of a fraud at any second. "The man and woman, they were married, Barry and Shirley Tonsworth. Seems like, when we looked through the records, we've had officers out here a couple of times on noise complaints. Called in by our friend Cain here."

Outside, Bradshaw heard the first drops of rain rattle against the window panes. He glanced off over his shoulder. He felt the temperature drop a couple of degrees and smelled that damp smell that rain brought. It was going to tip it down. He was sure.

Horowitz set his hands on his hips and looked over the pile of bodies. He released a long sigh. "Look, it's all straight-forward, right? I mean, Ipso and Facto"—he nodded to Peach Cheeks and Cherub Features, who hovered about by the door to the scene, clearly not quite wanting to take those police baby steps onto, what appeared to be, their first murder scene—"they could stitch this thing together from the information we've got."

He reached up and scratched his thinning hair, and Bradshaw caught sight of dozens of flakes of dandruff. "I mean, come on, Cain here, he's sick and tired of the noise up here, right, so he thinks, 'Well I've got a pretty nice big knife here, why don't I just go and run it through one or both's lungs and have an end to it once and for all?'"

Bradshaw grunted.

"And, well, that'd be all fine and dandy, hunky-dunkie dorrie, if you'll excuse the twee." Horowitz looked to Bradshaw. "Guess you know the problem though?"

"No weapon?"

"That's it. Nothing in sight. Not a damn clue of any sort. And the fact that, well, Cain did himself over here, stabbed himself through then threw himself down here, it just doesn't add up. What usually happens—what with all the cases I've studied, all the cases I've *seen* like this one—is the murderer does the deed then sneaks off somewhere else, has a guilt trip and then does himself in in some sort of privacy." He shook his head. "Doesn't usually throw himself down with the victims, not like this."

Bradshaw drew closer to the bodies, looking over Cain this time. He had to admit that Horowitz had done a fair job of deduction here, he was sure he could see a faint half smile on

Cain's lips, that kind of psychopathic satisfaction he'd seen so often on dead killers' faces, when they'd chosen their own demise. And then he looked to where he'd been stabbed. Between the ribs, right through the heart. A difficult trick to do himself, that was for sure. Could it be that either Barry and Shirley Tonsworth wrestled the knife off him and, perhaps with their dying breath, managed to strike back? Possibly. But, if so, where was the weapon? Just as Horowitz said, it would been extremely improbable, if not impossible, that someone in the state of dying from a knife wound would have the time, let alone the presence of mind, to get up and stash the weapon somewhere before returning to land in a fairly ordered heap. Not that he could rule it completely out. Yet.

Bradshaw sauntered out to the door of the flat, his heeled boots echoing about him.

"Where you going?" Horowitz said.

Bradshaw looked back over his shoulder briefly. "There a chemist near here?"

"Think I saw one on the corner."

Bradshaw nodded and stepped out into the now-driving rain.

3

HAVING REFUSED the offer of a ride from Peach Cheeks—he'd made it from the shelter of the flat, calling down those steps, Bradshaw walked alone in the rain, listening to his boots make wet slaps against the sodden pavement. The rain dripped off the rim of his hat. He could feel water seeping in through the crown and dampening his skull. He sniffed, feeling his cold worsen. He was getting that horrible swirling, gut-wrenching feeling too. If he'd had his way he might be sitting on a bus now, a nice warm one, stretched out on the backseat, hat resting over his eyes. But he was needed.

The chemist was a youngish woman with curly brown hair. She served him with a smile which was pretty nice. He was used to all those sidelong glances, the mothers hurrying their children away from him while they glanced back over their shoulders to make sure he hadn't been an optical illusion.

The chemist recommended him a bunch of sweets to suck. She told him to take a couple every he-forgot-how-many hours. He paid her then ventured back out into the pouring rain. She called after him. "You know you can stay here till it stops if you like, we don't charge for parking."

He glanced back at her, saw her smile and he smiled in return. "Don't have a car," he said, then he doffed his hat to her and ventured out, back through the rain.

The drops splattered against his leather jacket. When they collected together into streams they streamed down him and splashed down onto the ground. He cracked open the foil and snapped out all of those pills. They tasted of all sorts of artificial fruits. He got grape, apple, some lemon here or there, and then, at the back of his mouth, he tasted that woody pine again—just like that woman's perfume.

Soon the sweets all melded together into a single blocky, stodgy mass, and the flavours were forgotten. He felt the medicine do its work, dulling his senses, taking care of that throbbing migraine, easing the pressure around his eyes, and even warming him a little inside his chest. He could still taste that dryness in his throat but at least now he didn't have the pain. As he walked along he felt himself drifting, like he was being carried on a thousand wings.

He returned to the scene, looked up at that house. He nodded to the officer standing at the tape and then, hearing Peach Cheeks, Cherub Features and Horowitz still upstairs, at the scene of the murder, he slipped around the house, deciding to check out Cain's flat.

Forensics, or whoever, had already been in here. Why wouldn't they have? The lock had been busted off and then the door kept shut with a chair propped up against it. Bradshaw pushed the chair out of the way and then crossed the threshold into Cain's flat.

Now feeling his mind fully caught in a swirl, drifting off downstream, stuck in some water weed and then swooshing back along, Bradshaw took in the place. It was neat and tidy. An accountant's place. He looked to the calendar. This month's picture featured a sun-flooded cathedral. There were several notes against the dates all written in a careful hand. There were no loops to the style, no circles for dots. It was all very much under control. Again, an accountant's calendar.

He moved through the house like a damp sheet, feeling his brain thudding against his skull, and the light and fuzzy sensation of the pills keeping him warm. He passed through a sitting room and then into a utility room. That was when he reached the door that led out into a boxy back garden. The grass here, of course, was well-trimmed. The fence was painted a light blue colour with no bird crap whatsoever. Something about that sent a chill down Bradshaw's spine.

And then there was the shed out back. Well, he was definitely going to need to have a look there. He depressed the door handle and stepped out onto the patio. The cement tiles were all perfectly set—he felt them completely sure beneath his feet. He approached the shed and ran his hand across the wooden door. The edge of the wood was splintered, like coarse hair. Probably the first evidence of slob-like behaviour he'd noted in Cain's flat.

A padlock hung from the latch. It was clasped shut.

"Couldn't find the key."

Bradshaw's heart rose in his throat. He twisted around to see Horowitz standing at the back door, fishing for something in his cheek with his tongue—no doubt some remainder of his breakfast. He took a step out into the tiny garden then nodded to the lock. "Searched the damn place top to bottom. No sign of it."

Feeling his heart slow, probably also soothed to some extent by the pills he'd taken, Bradshaw looked over the shed again. "You didn't think to just bust it open, like the front door?"

Horowitz gave a half smile. "Nah, we've got—"

Bradshaw shoulder barged the door. It buckled under his weight, the wood cracked but didn't give way. He gave it another go. And then another. A crack appeared down the middle of the door. Bradshaw brought his foot up, his boot primed. Horowitz murmured something else but it was curtailed by the almighty *crunch* as he split the door in two.

One side remained held up by the hinges while the other clattered off into the shed, landing with a wooden *slap*, and sending up plumes of dust. Bradshaw caught just the vague suggestion of wood in his nostrils and on his tongue. He listening to the aftershocks, some wooden planks in the shed still creaking away. And then it was all still.

Horowitz sidled up to Bradshaw's shoulder. "Well, I'll sort out the paperwork on that one later, shall I?"

It was dark inside. When Bradshaw took a step forward the wooden planks creaked beneath his feet. He had to duck so as not to bump his head on the roof. He made out a few shapes in the gloom: a bicycle wheel with bent spokes, a blender with a broken plastic chamber and a battered old bucket, half-filled with filthy water. There was a retractable ladder stuffed carelessly into the rafters of the shed. So this was where Cain had hidden all his sloppiness, all his slobby tendencies.

"Anything interesting?" Horowitz said.

Bradshaw didn't reply, continuing to paw through the various pieces of junk: a rusted spanner, accompanied by several bolts in a similar state and then a tin of paint which, when Bradshaw tapped the side, sounded completely empty. There was a hook too. Nothing hanging from it though.

He checked over the place another couple of times but couldn't find anything interesting, nothing that might contribute to their understanding of the murder. Still, this place might come in useful later on, seeing as this was clearly where Cain kept another side of himself.

"Where you going?" Horowitz said.

Bradshaw didn't reply that time either, stalking his way past, mind seeming to blend into his bloodstream as he went. As he stood in the doorway of the shed he did notice something, though. He was surprised he hadn't noted it straight away. He crouched down to get closer.

There was a single clean circle on the shed floor, where something had once stood. Bradshaw frowned then reached over to touch the floor itself. As he brushed his fingers together he saw that there was a light layer of dust. Whatever had been there previously had only recently been moved.

He made eye contact with Horowitz and Horowitz, what with that cop sensibility, took that as a sign for him to get close and take a look for himself. The two them, Bradshaw crouched, like a folded antelope, and Horowitz half bent over, hands on his knees, like a cricket umpire. "What do you reckon was there?" Horowitz said.

Bradshaw blinked, feeling his eyelids growing heavy, a tiredness drooping itself over him. He crunched his eyes shut then straightened up, not wanting to give up right now—not while they were on the cusp of something. When he spoke his words took on a floaty quality, seemed to waft away from him on his breath. "Whatever it was I think we'll find it's the key to the murder."

As he stepped out of the shed, he found himself stumbling, and the last thing he remembered was falling to his side, his head smashing up against the kneecap-high brick wall which guarded the flowerbeds.

4

IT WAS NIGHT TIME when Bradshaw came to. Or, no it wasn't. The clouds had just darkened overhead. Whereas earlier there'd been a shower, now the main act was ready to fall on them. An all-out storm. He saw Peach Cheeks, Cherub Features and Horowitz all staring down at him.

Bradshaw rubbed his head, and looked out beyond them, first to the house, to that window in the flat above—the murder scene. And, as he looked out there, he saw some motion, something shifting its way along the wall. When he looked again it was gone.

He used his elbows to wriggle himself back up.

"Goodness!" Peach Cheeks said. "You were out for about ten minutes. Called an ambulance. It's on its way now."

Bradshaw tried to vocalise but he just managed another of his growls. He stumbled from one side to the other, eyes still fixed upward to that window of the flat above. But he saw nothing. Nothing remarkable.

His brain slopped about in his skull as he put one foot in front of the other.

"Take it easy, eh?" Horowitz said. "Maybe you should sit for a while—till the ambulance gets here."

This time Bradshaw managed to shake his head. He looked back over his shoulder and, through gritted teeth, said, "No ambulance. Call it off."

The three policemen all exchanged glances between themselves, but Bradshaw didn't care. He was right on the cusp here, the cusp of solving this thing and going . . . well, he didn't have a home to go to, so to speak. But he *was* on the cusp of getting away.

He stumbled through the house, that sickly too-clean scent of the place almost overwhelming. He could still smell that designer cologne at the back of it all—no doubt what Cain would've dabbed on himself before barrelling out through the door to work each day. He heard a clock ticking, a grandfather clock. He knew that steady beat of the pendulum anywhere. Although he remembered very little of his youth, he did have a very sure memory of a grandfather clock somewhere in his family home, and having gone to sleep more than once with that unending *tic-toc* thick in his ears.

In the hall, the place he just about skirted through first time around, sure that forensics would've given it a fair sweep, he spotted a cylindrical cage, one of those old wire bird cages. However, what marked it out from the rest of the house, everything he knew about Cain, was the soot sticking to it, turning those otherwise steel-grey wires a jet-black. He limped over to it, feeling a bruise forming on his shin where he supposed he must've hit it against something when he'd fainted. He brushed his fingertips against the cage. Just as he suspected, he came away with a thick coating of dust. This was something that Cain would never have stood for. And what was more, that cylindrical cage fit perfectly in that vacated space back in the shed. He was beginning to put the pieces together.

Like an itchy rash, he heard the voices of the police, Horowitz speaking in hurried tones with the two officers. Bradshaw rolled his eyes. His tongue felt thick in his mouth, all dried out, and there was a slight ringing in his ears. He wiped his dirtied fingers on the pockets of his trousers and then faced up to them, giving them the explanation they craved.

Back upstairs, in the flat above, Bradshaw jumped at the scene with fresh relish. He took in all the angles and, right at the end of his sweep of the room, he noted that window with the broken latch again. He spun round to face Horowitz. "That like that when the officers showed up?"

Horowitz shrugged.

Typical. When it came down the important stuff the police never had the answers. Then again that was why they'd called him in. To do the work they couldn't. From here on out he would be alone—it always got like that at this stage of a case.

He shifted over to the window, hoiking himself up onto the counter. He stuck his head out the window and examined the wall at either side. He was *sure* he'd seen something up here. And he was certain that if he was just patient he might—

Then there was motion around the corner of the wall. A brief second. A fleeting glimmer. Not long enough for Bradshaw to really be sure what it had been. The more he thought about it, tried to put form on his vision, he thought he'd seen a miniature human—a tiny person. It couldn't be.

Bradshaw took in his surroundings and noted the drainpipe which ran horizontal along the roof above him. He stepped out onto the window ledge.

"Hey!" Horowitz called out from behind him. "If you want to go out there we can call you in a cherry picker."

Bradshaw paid no attention to him as he reached out and tested the drainpipe for resilience. He yanked it a couple of times toward him, seeing if it would take his weight. He thought it might, for a little while anyway.

And so he grappled his fingers around the edge of the drainpipe, feeling the sharp edge of the plastic digging into his palms. With his feet he got some purchase on the odd brick that stuck out, taking as much strain off the drainpipe as he could. Soon enough, he reached the corner of the house, and prepared to turn it. Without needing to look back over his shoulder, he knew, instinctively, that the two police officers and the detective were leaning out that window and staring at him. No doubt they thought he was a lunatic. But he wasn't. He just got the job done. Was prepared to see things they refused to, and to go to the lengths to see them through that the common person just wasn't.

He swung himself around the corner, taking a tighter grip of the drainpipe. He felt a wind blow, tugging at his hat. A couple of drops fell onto his bare face and he blinked them out of his eyes. This storm was on the point of bursting and he needed to get this thing done, find out whatever the hell this thing was and intercept it.

He kept shuffling along, making his way along that drainpipe. And then he saw the motion up ahead, again on the periphery of his vision. His muscles strained and he heard the drainpipe creak beneath his grasp. This time he looked down to see the shed, the garden below him. But, more directly below, where he'd fall if he let go—or the drainpipe gave way—he saw the cement tiles. That would mean a broken leg, perhaps some broken ribs depending on how he landed. It would slow him down, that was for sure.

Finally he reached the next corner of the roof and peered around it. There, at the top of the gutter, the opening which resembled a funnel, he made out a furry head peering out at him. A monkey's face. Bradshaw held on tighter, feeling like his fingers had caught fire, what with the plastic digging in. They stared one another out for another couple of seconds before, with a grin, the monkey vanished down into the funnel section of the drainpipe. He reappeared a moment later clutching a blade, long and sharp, which he swatted through the air like a sword.

Bradshaw's heart caught in his throat and he felt that plastic become like the edge of a razorblade. His head pounded and he felt himself growing dizzy once more.

The monkey prowled out from its place in the funnel section of the drainpipe, clutching the knife in its grasp. It walked toward

Bradshaw on two feet, slowly approaching him as it came. Bradshaw backtracked a little, his body now feeling like a sack of potatoes. He wanted to call out, but was afraid that a sudden movement like that might either set the monkey on him or startle himself so much that he'd lose concentration and tumble down to the distant ground.

Working quickly, moving hand over hand, he managed to get himself back around the corner, about a quarter of the way back to the window—how he had got out here in the first place. More drops of rain fell. He felt the plastic of the drainpipe grow slippery. A stiff gust of wind caught the brim of his hand and tore it from his head. He felt the breeze blow his long, thin greasy black hair all about him. But the monkey continued to advance.

Below him he was aware of a scraping sound, metal on concrete, but he didn't dare look back, all his concentration fixed on the approaching monkey. Bradshaw shuffled his way along another few metres and then found he could go no further. It just hurt too much. The rain was falling steadily enough that the drainpipe was now lubricated, insufficient as a grip now.

His mind blanked out in the moment he was sure his burning fingers would fail him and he would tumble down, smashing himself on the concrete below. The monkey was only a matter of paws away from him now, a steady swipe of its knife would cut him, and he was sure he wouldn't be able to stand the pain. Staring at the monkey, its animal, indifferent features staring back at him, Bradshaw closed his eyes and let go.

5

BRADSHAW'S STOMACH sank as he fell. He prepared himself to drop onto the cement below, prepared himself for the flash of pain, and the dull pain that would follow, the weeks he might spend in a hospital being seen to by doctors and nurses, tutted over, and asked just where *exactly* it was that he lived. Whether or not he had any loved ones that they might contact.

But it didn't happen. Bradshaw felt solid support beneath his feet. When he looked down, finally getting a grip on himself, he saw Cherub Features standing below, holding up the retractable ladder which now supported him—had stopped him tumbling down. He gripped the rungs of the ladder with stiff fingers and, only having a moment to relish his improbable survival, turned his attention back upward.

The monkey, too, seemed a touch perplexed by this turn of events. But only for a moment, because it moved its fragile body, knife still in hand, and outstretched a tentative leg for the rung of the ladder. Then it shifted the knife into one hand and climbed down onto the next. And then the next.

Soon enough Bradshaw found himself caught up in a race. He willed his burning fingers to regain sensation, to help him down the ladder. He felt the soles of his boots slip more than a few times as he climbed down. And then, seeing himself only a couple of metres from the ground, he took a risk and leaped, landing with a thud on the now-damp grass.

The monkey increased its speed, pattering down the ladder. There wasn't enough time for Bradshaw to warn Cherub Features, and the monkey took a final bound, leaping at him with the blade outstretched. It seemed to happen in slow motion, the swing of the knife catching Cherub Features in the chin. Cherub Features buckled backward, falling down onto the same grass as Bradshaw, more out of shock than from the physical force of the monkey, and they became locked in a battle—Cherub Features somehow managing to seize hold of the monkey's knife hand and keep it from administering the killing stroke.

Bradshaw crawled his way back onto his feet and ran for the shed. He took a couple of seconds deciding once inside. He bounded over to the bucket of foul water, tipped it out, and then rushed back out. He watched on as the monkey extricated its wafer-thin wrist from Cherub Features's hold and drew back the blade, ready to bring it down into his chest, just as he had with the other three victims.

That was when Bradshaw struck. First knocking the monkey out of the way with the bucket, before dropping it over the maniacal animal and then holding it down with his firm hold. He listened to the *tinkle* of the blade against the inside of the bucket and brushed the thin layer of sweat from his forehead with the back of his hand.

6

ANIMAL CONTROL arrived half an hour later. They took special care to transfer the monkey, removing the knife from its sure grip as they did so, to a cage before sticking it into the back of their van and driving away. Peach Cheeks and Horowitz saw to Cherub Features's treatment, getting that rather nasty cut on his chin all patched up.

More officers arrived, the mystery now solved, and an estate car with tinted windows rolled up to take the dead bodies away. The officers were like flies on a cowpat, as they wandered in and out of the scene—looking for a pat on the head for uncovering some unimportant periphery detail. It was Peach Cheeks, however, who approached Bradshaw, Horowitz and Cherub Features while they sat about on Cain's sofa set.

He had the calendar clenched in his fist and was looking very pleased with himself. "Look," he said, holding it out, passing it in Horowitz's direction.

Horowitz took it from him then frowned. He flashed a look up at Peach Cheeks. "Mind helping an old man out here—what you kids've got to remember is that I never went to one of those posh universities."

Peach Cheeks looked to Bradshaw, who gave him an equally blank look, although, to be fair, Bradshaw's mind was mostly focussed on his next bus ride, getting out of here as soon as possible, back onto the road sounded good.

"It's a list of venues," Peach Cheeks said.

"Venues for what?" Horowitz said.

"Monkey knife fights."

"You're joking."

Peach Cheeks shook his head, grinning to himself. "Nah, I'm

sure of it—we should get people on it right away. Look at the times: midnight, one in the morning. These places are all provincial, out in the sticks, places that cops aren't likely to go without a tip off. This guy, Cain, he was well into the scene. In fact, I radioed back to HQ and got a couple of reports on these places—and guess what?"

"What?" Horowitz said, sounding just a little jaded.

"They've busted up fights before—monkey fights, cock fights, you name it, a ton of these places have reputations already. But this thing gives us the key. Tells us exactly when they're going to happen."

Horowitz shook his head and handed the calendar back to Peach Cheeks. "And to think the bastard kept the poor monkey in that damn shed this whole time. If what you say's true," he said, nodding to Peach Cheeks, "then he must've just been waiting for the opportunity, biding his time, ready for the right moment to set that monkey on his neighbours." He scratched his flaky scalp, sending a fresh storm of dandruff up into the air. "Guess he didn't account for it being so difficult to bring the animal back in, guess he thought it'd just damn well drop the knife, leap back into his arms. Then I guess it got scared, busted the latch off that window and hid out in the gutter."

Bradshaw remained steeped in silence, not really having anything else to add to the conversation. They had all the facts now and they could make of them whatever they wanted. It wasn't his place to stomp over this triumphant outpouring of explanation.

He got to his feet, feeling more of a sapling than the mighty oak he sometimes thought of himself. He was sure that a stiff breeze would have a fair chance at knocking him over, not just his hat next time. He made his way out, headed for the front door.

"Uh," Horowitz said, "where you headed?"

Bradshaw glanced back over his shoulder, back to the officers and the detective. They reminded him of school children struck into some sort of reverence. He wasn't anyone to admire. He just noticed the details—had a knack of seeing the things that others just didn't see for themselves. "Bus station."

"One of these two'll drive you, I'm sure," Horowitz said.

7

O N THE DRIVE BACK to the bus station, Bradshaw turned down the offer to sit in the passenger seat, even though Cherub Features had stayed behind. He thought the stench of baby powder up front might just be too much for him to handle.

He watched out of the window, looking into the grey streets passing them by, the umbrellas unfolded and their holders all passing by in a colossal hurry.

"Really is tipping it down, huh?" Peach Cheeks said, eyeing Bradshaw in the rear view mirror.

Bradshaw sniffed, finally feeling the earlier symptoms of his cold shifting. That dry blood taste that had lingered in his mouth had gone and that steady sense of satisfaction—at having solved a case—was beginning to dawn on him. He didn't answer Peach Cheeks.

They arrived back at the bus station without another peep between them. Bradshaw sat there, continuing to stare out the window, to the row of buses all lined up there, the exhaust fumes rising up against the mist of rain falling over everything, adding to the already-large puddles.

Peach Cheeks tapped his fingers against the steering wheel making a slightly annoying *tap-tap* rhythm, that plastic click that sincerely got on Bradshaw's nerves. He caught Bradshaw's eye in the mirror again. "Listen, I know this is going to sound personal, or whatever, and forgive me for prying, but—"

"No," Bradshaw said, meeting his eye. "Sorry, kid, I know you've got a good heart, but no thanks."

"Oh," Peach Cheeks said, then smiled vaguely.

"Really, I'll be fine. And don't think I get these offers a lot, and don't think that I'm not grateful for every last one of them—what with you kind people wanting to take me in, have me as an uncle, or a grandfather, more likely. But this is my life. This is where I'm at."

Peach Cheeks nodded glumly then pouted a little. "All right, then," he said. "Have a safe journey, I suppose."

They waited like that in silence for a little while. The police radio burbled loudly, something that Bradshaw didn't catch, or perhaps it was something that he just didn't want to hear. Peach Cheeks glanced back uneasy over his shoulder. "Waiting for the rain to stop, eh?"

The rain did patter down on the roof of the car, and streamed down the windows in rivulets. Bradshaw could hear it splash into puddles beneath the car.

"No," Bradshaw said. "I'm waiting for you to open the door."

Peach Cheeks remembered himself, swore under his breath, and dragged himself out of his seat, out of the car and to the back door which he opened for Bradshaw.

As Bradshaw stepped out, taking care not to knock his head on the roof as he went, he noted the flush growing in Peach Cheeks's . . . cheeks. He laid a steady hand on his shoulder and looked him in the eye. "Thanks for the lift, kid," and then he trod his way, slowly, through the deep puddles, right over to the waiting bus, the one which would leave at the earliest possible moment.

With the sound of the rain coming down harder, Bradshaw boarded. He took in the familiar smell of the warm upholstery, reached out and touched the headrests of the seats, squeezing each lightly as if it were a favourite grandson, and then took up that long-promised place across the backseat of the bus. He laid his head back with that dank taste of rain in his mouth and shovelled his hands back behind his head to form a pillow.

The rest just flowed away from him as if he was caught in a strong current, in a stream. And he felt himself leave the bus station behind and move on to the next town. The next town that needed him.

DEATH AND THE DUCHESS

1

SNOW FLUTTERED DOWN outside the window of the Spirit Room Bookshop. If Carol listened carefully she could hear the flakes gently brushing against the windowsill. She watched the flakes settling into dunes at either side of the street. The snowfall had eased off in the last half an hour. It would be a long walk back to her hotel, a tidy B&B in the centre of the town, that was for sure.

As she stared out at those freezing grey skies outside she found herself shivering a little despite her lambs-wool coat, the gentle stroke of its texture against her skin. She turned away from the window and regarded the room set out before her. The bookcases all jammed full with books, some were piled up against the walls where there was no room. All the books were second-hand, or in some cases third or fourth-hand. Their hard covers were scuffed round the edges and their golden lettering long faded. There must've been hundreds, thousands of them, all in this fairly small front room of the bookshop.

She *had* to find it here, somewhere among these hundreds of thousands—or were there millions?—of yellowing pages.

Who was she kidding? It was impossible. There were only a couple of hours before the shop closed its doors till Monday and she wouldn't find what she was looking for in that time. Then she would have to be back at work, working her way through the city legal system, and a fledgling barrister just couldn't afford not to turn up. This solitary Sunday afternoon had been all she could tease out from her otherwise hectic schedule. Never before in her life had she felt so hopelessly lost, powerless to do anything.

When she noticed the figure standing in the doorway her heart rapped a couple of dozen times rapidly. Then she saw it was only the kindly bookshop owner, the man in his seventies, or maybe eighties. He was at that age where it became impossible to tell age exactly. He had wrinkled, leathery skin. A hooked nose. She saw that he held a steaming mug in his hands, hot chocolate she could tell from the smell. He smiled at her then said, "You just take your time, love, don't you worry." He paused, as if stuck in thought for a second, that way that old people did, it reminded Carol of when a dodgy second-hand car stalled and its ignition had to be turned over a dozen times before it got up and running again. He squinted at her. "You look familiar to me, very familiar. Have you been in here before?"

Carol shook her head, and smiled faintly. "No," she said. "First time I've come here in my whole life."

The man parted his lips a little, then shook his head and held the mug out to her.

Carol took the mug off him and sipped the chocolate. And the hot gooiness of it warmed her all the way through. Almost made her forget about the snow outside. About what she desperately needed to find.

Almost.

2

BRADSHAW PEELED BACK his seatbelt and peered out from beneath the windscreen of the police car. He saw the building in cinders, right out there before him, barely a few feet of burned-out wall left standing. There were still puddles of grey water collected about the wreckage. About what had once been the Spirit Room Bookshop.

His whole body ached. It had been a long ride over. The nearest bus station to this place was a clear thirty-minute drive away. Of course there were rural services, but, like always, the police insisted on picking him up themselves, and, in any case, rural services only ever seemed to run buses about once every other blue Moon.

He stepped out of the police car and surveyed the scene. As he stood there, his hand resting on the chilled shell of the car, he felt the snowflakes coming down and brushing up against his skin, sending a slight shudder around the collar of his leather jacket. He could still smell the smoke in the air. That strange mixture of the cold—almost numbing—snowfall, and that scent of burned paper. He could taste that ash fill his nostrils, his mouth, layer itself onto his tongue.

He listened to the driver's door slam shut and he peered out over the roof of the police car, over the smooth, well-polished charcoal-coloured paintwork, to the detective on the other side— the detective who had picked him up from the bus station, the detective who had a case that he simply couldn't solve.

The detective had those deep, sea-green eyes. Just the types of eyes that can spell disaster for anyone caught up in any big trouble. Kind eyes. Innocent eyes. Bradshaw wondered if the detective had a family at home, a wife and kids. He guessed he did. Perhaps a boy and a girl, a wife with thick, blond, curly hair and a buxom figure. But Bradshaw had no intention of confirming any of these gut assumptions. Because he only knew that it would turn attention back towards himself. And he had no intention of telling *anyone* about his past.

As the detective stood leaning up against the closed driver's door, Bradshaw took in the bookshop, or what remained of the bookshop, another time.

There were piles of books, reduced to pulp, which the firemen had taken out when they'd got through with this place. They were all standing resting up against the foundations of the brick walls, against the charred bricks that looked close to toppling over at any second. Bradshaw wondered what kind of insurance this place had, and that started him off on other tangents, other possibilities, wondering whether the bookshop owner might've been attempting to commit insurance fraud. But it wouldn't be anything that clean—nothing that simple. Else the police wouldn't have bothered getting in touch with him at all.

The detective rubbed his hands together and his breath came out in clouds as the snow fell harder. He glanced over at Bradshaw, and Bradshaw knew immediately that he was attempting to avoid his gaze, that was how people acted with him, and considering that he was a smidge over six foot six, and he liked to dress in a trench coat with a wide-brimmed matching black hat, he supposed he couldn't blame *people*.

When the detective spoke he had a slight raised pitch to his voice, as if he was constantly on the edge of asking a question, but he held back each time. Perhaps he was afraid to put a foot wrong. Perhaps, like a lot of these cops, he was afraid of being shown up, having had to call Bradshaw in to bear on his case. "So, getting a little dark now."

Just a pure, simple statement, and yet again a faint hint of an implied question. Just like whenever he spoke. Bradshaw gazed to the skyline, above the burned-out bookshop and smiled slightly. He was right. The sun *was* dipping in the sky. The clouds were getting plump and billowy. Soon the streetlights would glint their orange glow about the place. In the matter of an hour or so it would be night-time. And, Bradshaw supposed, this detective wanted to get back to his wife and kids. Away from whatever hideousness it was that he was wrapped up in.

Bradshaw thought back to the car ride over. He could always tell just what type of cop he was dealing with on the car ride from the bus station—where they always picked him up from. They would either blabber about the case in that cocksure way that cops do, or else they'd stay silent. And he knew that the former were the experienced ones, and the latter the ones that were a little shell-shocked by the whole thing, not to mention confused. But this detective, he had been different. He had laid out the matter, explained it to him, and then left it there. No boasting, no speculation, no hint of excitement *or* nervousness at the prospect of a solved case. Bradshaw was coming to believe that, for this detective, his job really was just a job. And he really did want to go home to those wife and kids of his.

Bradshaw shifted round the bonnet of the unmarked car, its paintwork just as gleaming black as the rest of it. As the snowflakes fell on it, he couldn't help thinking that it was sullying the car in some way, making it dirty. Not that Bradshaw cared. Cleanliness was just another thing, another complication that didn't need all that much paying attention to. Unless it was some-thing of a suspect he was trying to fathom.

He had a rule of never answering questions about the weather. But this detective hadn't asked him a question at all. He'd hinted at it, but never made it, and so Bradshaw wouldn't waste any words on him.

He stepped over the soggy, slushy street, and paced up along the stomped garden path—a series of stones all buried into the frozen earth—and he stepped over the threshold, and into the house. He had little interest whether or not the detective followed him.

Inside the bookshop, if it could be said to be inside, since the whole roof had burned off in the fire, Bradshaw strode between the gutted rooms, where the firemen had blasted the furnace into submission. He inspected the marks on the walls, the sooty stains that still remained there, despite having been exposed to the elements for several hours. As he trod, he could hear the groan and creak of the wooden floorboards beneath his feet.

Ash still floated in the air, pages of books incinerated in the fire lingered there like a fine mist. He breathed them in, tried to see what it might tell him, but it only irritated his sinuses and the back of his throat, and he felt the urge to sneeze rising up to his nose. He sniffed it back then walked on.

He arrived in the room which the detective had informed him the firemen had deduced to be the source of the fire. It was a small, tight front room of the bookshop, with what remained of shelves—cindered planks of pine wood—rested up against the walls. He reached down and brushed his fingertips against the fire damage, trying to see back to the fire, trying to visualise. This was the room where they'd found the two bodies.

His muscles ached as he crouched down there. He always felt awkward, cumbersome, when he was close to the ground, and here he felt no different. He sucked in deep breaths, taking in yet more ash and, this time, snowflakes. That fiery, icy chill passed through him, and he thought he could hear screaming, loud, almost piercing in his ears. And then he pushed it away. He never liked to rack his brains too hard, to imagine things too vividly, it brought him too close to his own—*distant*—pain.

He rose back up and examined the room yet again. When he glanced back over his shoulder he saw the detective standing there, looking on, a vacant expression on his face. He was beaten. He had no idea just what he needed to be looking for here. One thing was for certain, they wouldn't have called Bradshaw in if this had been a simple case of a house fire, even an arson. The allegation being bandied about here was murder. Someone had set the fire to *murder* the two people.

When Bradshaw wrestled himself into the detective's gaze, he was surprised the detective had the strength to speak to him. "Morgue?" the detective said.

Bradshaw grunted in reply, then brushed the ash from his jacket, his long, gnarled fingernails making a zipping sound as they scraped his leather trench coat.

3

ANOTHER FIFTY MINUTES LATER, leaving the bookshop well behind, and they arrived at the morgue, where the two bodies had been brought. Bradshaw kept his teeth clenched together on the ride over, not wanting to be the one to break the silence in the car. He never did like talking all that much.

The two bodies lay on white-sheeted beds in a room which was almost as cold as it was outside. Bradshaw shook his head when offered a face mask and latex gloves by the mortician and he just ventured on inside.

The chemical tang hung in the air and Bradshaw felt that stench of ash finally being torn from his body and replaced by something much more artificial, something stronger. He listened to a drip coming from across the room. When he looked over, he saw a large glass jar of amber liquid, its sprout constantly dribbling into an ever-growing pool on the tiled floor. It reminded him a little of diluted blood. Maybe that was what it was. He hadn't all that much knowledge about morgues and little interest in finding out more.

The mortician led them over to the two bodies. One a woman, Bradshaw could only tell by the rise of her chest beneath the sheet. "Miss Buckleman," the mortician said, his breath catching for just a second. He shook his head. "Looks so much like her grandmother."

Then he moved over to an old man, concealed beneath the other sheet and peeled it back. "Mr Harbourberry."

Bradshaw drew closer to get a good look. Both of their features were melted into indistinct masses of flesh and bone, it reminded Bradshaw of what would happen when you left a bag of hard-boiled sweets out in the sun. He couldn't help but stare at their faces. Bradshaw chanced a quick sidelong look at the detective, trying to get a read on him. But nothing. He showed no emotion whatsoever. Just blank detachment.

The mortician coughed to get their attention. It worked. He was a miniscule man, with thin-framed spectacles, and pallid, almost milk-white skin. He had thick liver spots on his forehead and his otherwise pristine apron had a bloody mark about an inch above the pocket in the front. He was almost bald, his wiry grey hair hanging about at his ears like low-lying, detached rain clouds on a bitter, cold winter's day. Even though he wore glasses he squinted at them as he spoke, as if even with that heavy prescription he had trouble seeing them.

"There was one thing," he said. "Something that I wanted to show you two. That is if you're finished here."

Bradshaw cast a glance back over the bodies, and then looked to the detective, who merely nodded. Bradshaw then, in turn, nodded to the mortician, who flitted round and led them from the morgue and out into an annexed room alongside.

Only as the chemical stench faded did Bradshaw even realise just how thick it had been in the air, back there with the bodies. He thought of the mortician's wife, wondered whether she noticed that stench any longer . . . then again, perhaps the mortician didn't have a wife at all. Maybe he lived on his own with a cat or two for company.

The room alongside the morgue was tight, barely enough room for the three of them to stand. In the centre of it was a steel table, which was shined-up so bright that Bradshaw could see a suggestion of his reflection staring back at him. The walls were occupied by lockers, substantial, oak wood lockers with old-style combination locks on each of them. Bradshaw supposed, this being a backwater kind of place, that they didn't have all that much in terms of budget round here. And, he supposed, that despite the age of the lockers, they were in pretty much mint condition. He guessed the mortician took a lot of care about this place, took pride in keeping it well-maintained. It was a living.

The mortician approached one of the lockers, kept his back facing them to block what his hands were doing, and he twisted the combination lock for a few seconds. Tiny clicks and snicks filled the air before the telling *sprong* as the mechanism gave way. The mortician dipped his hand inside and brought out a tattered, clearly burned-up book. It was almost cinders it was so beaten up, but, Bradshaw saw, he could just about make out the matter on the front of it. As the mortician held the book in his hands at his chest, Bradshaw read the title:

Death and the Duchess

Bradshaw glanced to the detective. Again, no reaction, not even the batting of an eyelid. Not even in the face of such a clue as this.

The mortician held onto the book tightly in his hands, with strength that suggested that if he dropped it, it would crumble into a thousand irrecoverable pieces. Bradshaw guessed that, really, he couldn't be far off with that assumption.

"She was clutching this to her chest," he said.

Bradshaw continued to inspect the book. He asked himself whether there was anything particular about it, if anything about it jumped out at him. But, no. All he could see there, held in the mortician's hands was a book. An old, pretty much burned up, book. He caught a whiff of that ash again, that unmistakable stench of burned pages, and then he met the mortician's eye, but Bradshaw didn't speak. He didn't see the point.

The mortician nodded vaguely then handed the book over to Bradshaw, who took it in his hands. He glanced to the detective, standing at his shoulder, wondering whether he was going to make some neurotic, cop-like remark about him having to put on some latex gloves so as not to damage the *evidence*. But the detective stayed quiet. Bradshaw had to admit that he was getting to like this guy more and more.

Bradshaw examined the book. *Death and the Duchess*. It wasn't in such a bad state as the other books back in the bookshop in that he could still make out the individual pages, could still turn the pages. Inside, though, the damage was more obvious. He could see where the flames had clawed at the printed pages, forever rendering them illegible. The cover page of the book, though, was still distinct. He could still make out the words written there. It was a repeat of the title, some author's name he couldn't recognise, and then he saw, written out as a subtitle, 'A Mystery.'

Again, he glanced back in the detective's direction, trying to see if he had anything useful to add to this. But the detective, yet again, just stayed quiet. Bradshaw looked in the mortician's direction, and the mortician looked just as devoid of ideas, not to say that it was his job, his *role*, to find out just what this meant. He was a mere guardian of the dead.

"You can keep the book," the mortician said, then turned back to close the locker door.

4

THEY DROVE ON, pounding into the countryside. Bradshaw stared out the window at the darkened landscape, all just about lit up in the dampened moonlight—snow coming down in sheets—and he felt a slight chill pass through the heating of the car. He glanced at the detective again, trying to read something there from his face in profile, and he finally got the urge to do something that he never, *ever* did. And before he could check himself he was already doing it. It was too late.

"Not gotta be back with wife and kids?" Bradshaw said.

The detective didn't respond for a moment or so, staring out at the road peeling out before them, keeping the wheel steady as he guided the car round the gentle bend, occasional strands of overgrown grass from the verges tickling Bradshaw's window. Then, still staring out ahead, the detective responded. "Nope."

Bradshaw left the conversation there, knowing when to just leave something alone. And he peered out through the windscreen, along with the driver, wondering just where they were going. Where they were headed.

In the course of leafing through the book, on the apparently aimless car ride, Bradshaw checked through the pages, reading off the story—or what he could of it from the remaining legible words. It concerned a Duchess, no surprises there, and it turned out that there was a murder at her house—an elegant, Edwardian-style manner located on, and referred to, as the Huxley Estate. As Bradshaw read on, onto the second page, he found out that it was the gardener who was the *Death* of the title. Gruesome too. The murderer, as yet unknown, had killed the gardener by shoving a hosepipe down his throat then switching it on full. And a pair of unlikely inspectors had been called in to deal with the investigation, and made to work out just how this gardener had got done in.

A few pages along the author teased out a pretty tedious explanation of how whoever had managed to kill the gardener had to have possessed a great amount of strength, been able to restrain the man, hold him down, while they shoved the pipe down his throat and flooded his lungs. This, apparently, ruled out the frail old duchess of the house, the man's employer, and, in any case, she had no motive for committing such a crime. From Bradshaw's experience, he knew that if rich people did want something like this getting done then it was almost a die-cast certainty that they'd pull it off. Money could buy you anything . . . if you knew the right people.

The whole mystery—the mystery from the title—came about from the only person being on the estate, being in the vicinity of the murder, was the duchess. The next living being was five miles away, snug in a valley that took a great deal of meandering down a hilly, rocky path and, anyway, had an alibi thoroughly absolving him of any suspicion. And so, it seemed, that it was, in fact, the duchess who'd committed the murder. But the question that plagued the two inspectors was the *how*.

Bradshaw had to admit that he was feeling the same. But as it turned out, the book ended there, at least for him. From that page onwards the text was completely lost to the ash, unreadable, and so he slapped the book shut.

He felt the car judder to a halt and the scuff of gravel beneath them. He felt the tattered old, half-destroyed book slip slightly in his grasp, but he caught it before it fully fell from his hands. He glanced over at the detective, looking for some explanation of just what had gone on. And then, seeing the man staring right out into the road ahead of him, Bradshaw turned to look too.

There, lit up in the flood of yellowy headlights was a man of about forty.

5

THE MAN SQUINTED into the headlights, holding his hand up over his eyes to shield them from the glare, clearly trying to make out the inside of the car. He wore a burgundy fleece and was shaped like a barrel, his cheeks were slightly rosy, Bradshaw first thought from the chilly, snowy air, but then, on second thought, he remembered glancing a pub a few miles back and so guessed that to be the real cause.

Bradshaw got a tingle right across his skin. He could feel the vibration of the car engine, ticking over, and hear it puttering away. He glanced to the detective, but he just kept staring straight ahead, those sea-green eyes seemingly dead and matted. Bradshaw left him behind and stepped out of the car.

The man swayed slightly as he took in Bradshaw, then he stumbled from one foot to the other. Bradshaw knew then that he'd been right in assuming the man was drunk. He abhorred drunks. Drunks disturbed his sleep at night, when he'd sleep on buses, drunks babbled incessantly, wept or started fights. His father had been a drunk.

The man manipulated his lips as if he had some kind of cotton mouth, then he said, "You? You?"

Bradshaw stood straight, making sure the man took in his entire height. That had a trick of intimidating people into talking sense. Even drunks sometimes.

The man then stumbled a few paces forwards, then held up his arm, guarding himself from the bright headlights. "*You!*"

Bradshaw remained where he was. He felt steady, calm, his heartbeat under control. He breathed in that fresh winter's night air, and tasted a few snowflakes that found their way into his mouth. As he surveyed the place he saw the iced-over fields, all of them glistening slightly in the moonlight. He withdrew held up his hands—red from the cold—to show the man that whatever harm he thought he was carrying, the man was mistaken.

As the man drew closer still, Bradshaw observed the deep-set redness of the man's face. That was a redness that not even a combination of seven or more pints and a snowy night-time walk could produce. He knew, just from looking at the man, that this was an ingrained habit of his. The man was an alcoholic.

The man squinted some more, past the headlights now, and only a few paces from Bradshaw. He was obviously trying to peel back the shadow concealing his face. "What you . . ." Another stumble to the right. "What you . . . doin'?"

Bradshaw just stared the man down. He'd heard what people called him, that they called him The Scarecrow, as if he didn't hear just what they said behind his back. But he knew, at the same time, that that was how he could be intimidating. And it served him to be intimidating now.

"You . . . You give me . . . a *lirrf* home?"

Bradshaw guessed the man had wanted to say 'lift' but the whisky, or whatever he'd been knocking back all night, had obscured that. He stayed just as still as before, waiting for the man to explain himself further.

The man drew even closer, so that Bradshaw caught a reek of the man's body odour, of the damp patch of drink spilled all down the front of his fleece. He'd been right about the whisky. That sour, malty smell seemed to pervade everything now, defiling the fresh winter air.

The man peeled his arm away from his side and pointed down the road, his fingers were stubby, like pork sausages, and just as greasy. "Down . . . down there." The man closed his mouth, his cheeks bulged as if he might be about to vomit, but the sensation—apparently—passed and he turned his full attention back to Bradshaw. "You take me? . . . Down in the valley."

Bradshaw stared the man down for the longest time, then he glanced back in through the car window, to the detective, both his hands still gripping the wheel, still staring ahead as if he hadn't even noticed the conversation taking place. Bradshaw tapped his knuckles against the glass and watched the detective turn to look at him. The detective gave him a single, firm nod, and Bradshaw helped the drunken man into the backseat of the car.

6

THEY RODE ON DOWNWARD, along the narrow, snaking lane, and into the valley the man had mentioned. Bradshaw kept his eyes firmly fixed on the rear-view mirror, making sure the man wasn't about to do something rash like yank back on the door handle and toss himself out. Not that it would've been that bad a thing for a *drunkard* like this man.

The man kept his hands to himself for the rest of the journey.

The detective pulled up outside a neat cottage precisely in the middle of nowhere. Bradshaw gazed out across the scene from the passenger seat. It was well-kept, its garden covered in snow dunes, and, a little further back, behind the house, he could see a frozen-over duck pond. Something about this place was familiar. But before he got the chance to raise any such issue, he noticed the drunken man leaning over from the backseat, staring at the book which Bradshaw had lying in his lap.

"De . . . Death and . . . tha . . . Duchess."

Bradshaw pivoted round in his seat and glared at the man, wishing him out of the car, away to his cottage to dream his drunken dreams, and to feel awful the next day. And yet, something told him that he might be onto a clue, that this case might not be all that far from being resolved.

The man blinked several times, then said, "You know, that's the story my granddad wrote, that is."

The detective stirred from his seat, turning round too. He joined Bradshaw in glaring at the man. "What?" he said, for the first time actually looking interested in the case.

Bradshaw allowed himself a wry grin, which the detective

had no way of seeing in the gloomy interior of the car. It escaped him how this drunkard had such great eyesight. He supposed that such gifts were wasted on people like that. That was the problem with gifts.

The drunken man eyed both Bradshaw and the detective, a little uncertainly, like a toddler trying to work out whether it has pleased or disgusted its parents. Then he turned back to look at the book. "*Death and the Duchess*, that's my granddad's book." He pointed off toward the cottage. "Family house, this is, come down through the generations. Just mine now since Dad moved down into town."

The detective narrowed his eyes. "When did your granddad write this book?"

The man shrugged. "Dunno, fifty years ago, maybe."

"Is he still alive?"

The man shook his head. "Nah, . . . *died*."

The detective turned back to Bradshaw, surely looking to him for some masterstroke. That was the thing with these police, whenever things got too tricky for them they always looked to him, whenever the line of enquiry got even the least bit sticky.

Still, Bradshaw checked out their surroundings again, thought back to what he'd read in the book, about a valley, a house all on its own, the neighbour living closest to . . . what was its name? . . . *Huxley Estate*, that was it.

The man continued, "That's a *true*, uh, uh, . . . *story*."

"What?" the detective said, flashing his eyes.

The man nodded, with an idiot grin spreading his cheeks. Then he pointed off up the hillside, above the cottage. "Huxley Estate's jus' . . . jus', 'bout, five miles or so that way."

Bradshaw pressed himself back into his seat, reached up and wiped a line of sweat forming about his hatband with his index finger. Then he glanced back at the man, but he had no need to ask the question, since the detective asked it for him.

"Can we come into your house?" the detective said.

BRADSHAW AND THE DETECTIVE stood over the man, sitting at his kitchen table, a cobbled-together wooden affair with several coffee cup rings all over the top of it and, Bradshaw noted, several red wine rings there too. The whole cottage was quaint. It had a smell of sawdust hanging about it, a light tang of vomit too, and everything seemed so sturdy and rustic, so much so that Bradshaw had no qualms about leaning back against a wooden rafter, seemingly holding up the whole roof. The rafter stuck down into the middle of the room getting in the way of everything, as aspects of old house designs are wont to do.

The man held the steaming cup of coffee between his podgy hands. Droplets of sweat seeped out of his skin and glistened in the crisp, white kitchen light. They were trying to sober him up, at least coffee had always worked with Bradshaw's father, when he could actually manage to get him to sit down and be quiet for a few moments. The scent of whisky and body odour seemed to thicken in the stifling kitchen air. Bradshaw assumed the man had left the heating on full-blast when he'd gone out to the pub.

The man took great big gulps of air, his throat echoing with each respiration and then his eyes bounced between Bradshaw and the detective as he sipped at the coffee.

"Well?" the detective said.

The man's Adam's apple bobbed as he gulped down another mouthful of coffee, then said, "It all happened, just like in the book. True, uh, crime."

The detective turned in Bradshaw's direction, and Bradshaw gave him a concise explanation, secretly bemoaning all the talking he had to do. He informed the detective that he hadn't been able to read any more of the story after the initial setup, that the text from there on was illegible. After Bradshaw had explained, the detective turned to the drunken man. "So, what happens at the end of the story? Who killed the gardener, then?"

The man hesitated several moments then broke out into a broad grin, his cheeks shining like a pair of glossy red apples. "Suicide."

"Suicide?" the detective said.

The man nodded. "Of course it was." His eyes sunk back in their sockets and he turned a shade paler. "How else could it happen?"

The detective looked to Bradshaw for answers again, surely wanting to know just what was going on now that he'd found himself in yet another dead end. Bradshaw guessed that he would need to step in now. He confronted the drunken man at the table, keeping his gaze cold, and the brim of his hat pulled down way low to cover his eyes. He *hated* it when people looked him in the eye.

"Girl and old man were killed in a fire," Bradshaw said, "back in town, in the bookshop, Spirit Room Bookshop. We're trying to find out who set the fire."

The man looked confused, his eyes almost swimming about his head. Bradshaw wondered just how much of this was going in. He guessed that it might take a lot more than a cup of coffee to unstew the man's brains.

"The girl"—Bradshaw grabbed hold of the book and shook it before the drunken man for effect—"she was holding this book. Why do you think that was?"

The man glanced to the detective, then to Bradshaw. He gave him an open-mouthed shrug, then knocked back the rest of his coffee. He brought the mug down with a porcelain *thud* on the wooden table top. "No . . . idea," the man said.

Bradshaw stood firm, telling himself that he had to stay calm, that he had to get all the information he could possibly squeeze from this specimen. "You said the story was based on a real story, tell us about that."

The man frowned. He looked a smudge less drunk now, like the coffee was having some effect. "What d'you wanna know?"

Bradshaw just breathed heavily through his nostrils, and that was all it took for the man to get on with what they wanted to know.

"My granddad, he . . . he used to, you know, go and, erm, . . . bring shopping to her—to the duchess."

Bradshaw arched an eyebrow, not that the man would be able to see it since he did it from beneath the brim of his hat.

"She got *old*." The man burped, caught his breath then continued. "Her husband died, or something."

"The duke," the detective said, glancing over in Bradshaw's direction.

Bradshaw really was growing increasingly surprised by the man's lapse out of lethargy. But with regards to that particular contribution he guessed it might've been better for the detective to keep his mouth shut. But, still, at least he was *trying* to get in on the act.

"My granddad, he'd go along, help her out. And she'd pay him for it."

Bradshaw looked over to the detective, to see if he was beginning to catch a clue, for Bradshaw this case was almost closed, and he knew that he was approaching his conclusion. But he liked to make cops feel good, if at all possible. After all, what would they do after he was dead and buried?

"What's your name?" Bradshaw said.

The man hesitated a moment, and Bradshaw could almost read his mind, see him thinking to himself that these two cops had burst into *his* home and now they were taking liberties, he was approaching that point where he would come to his senses and chuck them out.

"Harold," he said.

"Harold, what?"

"Harold Yaughtsman . . . Harold Yaughtsman Junior if you wanna be pedantic about it."

Bradshaw looked over to the detective, who had silently produced a notebook and was scribbling that down. There was just one more thing that this man could help them out with, something that would simply solidify things in Bradshaw's mind, *truly* wrap up the case. And so Bradshaw dished it out without any further delay. "The duchess," he said. "What was her name?"

The man kept his gaze steady, between the two of them, and then shifted off to look into mid-air. For the first time in their whole acquaintance there was a sort of gravity about him—an assuredness. And then he said, "Duchess Buckleman."

That was just what Bradshaw wanted to hear, and with that he tore out of the house, listening to the steady footsteps of the detective following him soon after.

8

BACK IN THE CAR, Bradshaw felt the coolness coming off the passenger seat window, the glass was almost iced over now on his side since they'd left the car outside the man's cottage. And he felt those familiar hunger pangs in his stomach, and that slightly sour taste at the back of his throat from that remainder of the whisky. He wanted to banish that smell from his nostrils forever more. He listened to the car engine hum along, its wheels crunching as they proceeded along the gravelly countryside road, and felt that same familiar tug towards sleep that he felt whenever he stepped onto a bus after a hard day's work. They were heading back towards the town.

Unsurprisingly the detective wanted to know just what had happened, to know the conclusions that Bradshaw had seemingly rushed into. But Bradshaw knew himself that he never, *ever* rushed to a conclusion. He just sat back, soaking up the facts, waiting for his moment to strike, like a venomous snake lying in wait in the grass. And now was the time to strike.

Bradshaw glanced over at the detective. "It's your lucky day, you've solved three murders in one go."

The detective frowned, still staring directly ahead.

"We've worked out who killed the gardener, all that time ago, and who killed the girl, Carol Buckleman, and the bookshop owner."

The detective stayed silent, although Bradshaw was almost certain that he thought he was about to say that it was the duchess had done it. That would've been just like a cop. And it would only have served to spook the true murderer, given him a chance at making a break for it.

"That girl, Carol Buckleman, I think we can assume that she

was the duchess's granddaughter, a name like Buckleman isn't something you hear every day, is it?"

The detective remained silent, hands just sliding fractionally every second or so to keep the car ploughing onwards, headed for the town.

"And so, it seems only natural that she might be looking for a book which featured her grandmother, don't you think?"

The detective looked at Bradshaw out of the corner of his eye. "Duchess Buckleman passed away about thirty years ago, the Huxley Estate is now opened by a charity, for anyone who wants to visit. She didn't die under mysterious circumstances, so why would her granddaughter come looking for answers?"

"Just out of interest. Wouldn't you go looking for a book if you knew that it featured one of your own relatives, mysterious death or not?"

The detective shrugged, and continued to grip the steering wheel firmly.

"Well, that's what Carol Buckleman did. I don't know, these aristocratic types are always bothered about their family history, so why would she be any different?"

The lights from the town below were beginning to glow at the end of the road. The snow shifted in and out of sight as it passed through the beam of the headlights, and Bradshaw got the familiar shudder through his chest, the shudder telling him that they were on the brink of solving the thing.

The detective slipped Bradshaw a sidelong glance. "How does that tell us who the murderer is, who started the fire?"

Bradshaw straightened his back and pressed himself into the smooth seat, that perfect mixture of rigidness and soft that he recognised from the buses. "The same person who killed the gardener with the hose pipe."

"Who?"

Bradshaw just kept himself pressed into his seat, enjoying the waves of warmth coming out from the car heater. His mouth felt parched but the good news was the stench of whisky was eking its way out from his system. And soon enough it would be gone completely. Then he said, in a husky whisper, "Do you know where Harold Yaughtsman Senior lives?"

9

THEY PULLED UP outside a terrace house painted a cream colour with violet shades for the window ledges and the borders. The door, too, was violet. Bradshaw sat in the passenger seat, eyeing the house, staring at those netted curtains concealing the interior, and the faint orange glow coming from one of the bedrooms up above. This would be an easy arrest for the detective. If he was lucky he would catch the man still in bed, blinking away that sleepiness. He probably wouldn't even put up a fight, he had to be in his sixties after all, and the detective was a strapping man of early middle age.

The detective, though, didn't stir from the driver's seat. He glanced to Bradshaw. "I want to be sure," he said. "The Yaughtsmans, they're an old family from around here, even if the son's a drunkard."

Bradshaw let loose a sigh and supposed he'd have to go through the whole lot with him, just to encourage him along. "Harold Yaughtsman Senior killed the gardener, and he killed Carol Buckleman, burned the bookshop to the ground to get rid of the book too. His father— Yaughtsman Junior's grandfather— wrote that true crime book as a kind of diversionary tactic, he put the thing together to absolve his son from any blame, when really, for whatever reason, he decided to kill Duchess Buckleman's gardener.

"Yaughtsman Senior saw Carol Buckleman wandering around the town, and from what the mortician says she's a dead-ringer for her grandmother, and so it seems a fair assumption that Yaughtsman Senior thought the same, put two and two together, then decided she, and the book, needed to be got rid of. To stop her from stumbling over the truth."

Bradshaw looked over the detective again, tried to meet his eyes—sometimes it was unavoidable, important to make sure the message had got across.

Then the detective, hunched over, clicked open the glove compartment, and removed a handgun from within. He checked it over in the weak interior car lamp light then stepped out, his footsteps crunching as they set down in the fresh snow and ice.

10

ABOUT TWO HOURS LATER, after Bradshaw had finished up with all the police business, shaken the hand of just about every member of the local constabulary, or so it seemed, he sat shivering on the sole wooden bench, at the bus terminal, waiting for a ride. As he felt a fresh, freezing northern breeze sting his cheeks, he heard that familiar throb of a bus engine, crawling its way slowly up the hill. And he turned to look.

The glare of the bus headlights hurt his eyes, but he didn't look away. He just stared at it as if he was staring right between the eyes of a ferocious animal. And before he knew it the bus pulled up alongside where he sat, its hydraulics hissing, and with the swing of its doors opening that welcoming warmth washed all over him.

And he knew he was home.

TIED TO LIFE, UNITED IN DEATH

1

RACHEL DANCED her way up the spiral stairs. Her body felt fragile, almost like a bird's. It was funny how her steps no longer seemed to carry any weight, that her muscles seemed to have limitless strength. She breathed the air, had to keep telling herself to breathe, and it stunned her how fresh it was, like the cleansing effect of drinking water. She could taste it washing her mouth clean too. She kept on up the steps, following the bright white light up there.

As she continued on her way she noticed the light *hum* that now seemed to throb through the air, dwindle in and out of her hearing. She stopped for a second, listened intently to it. Come to think of it she couldn't be sure whether she heard the hum at all. Maybe she was just imagining it.

Was she just imagining all of this?

She felt her mind growing perplexed as she continued her way up the ever-spiralling stairs, the corkscrew wind, heading right up to that incredibly—*celestially*—bright light and she knew that she had never been this hopelessly lost in all her life.

And then the darkness got in again.

That *damn* darkness.

She only realised her eyes were open when she observed the sallow little circle of torchlight pass over her vision.

Rescuers?

Perhaps . . .

Where had *that* thought come from?

Why did she need *rescuing?*

And then, moment by moment, second by second, it all returned to her.

She could almost feel her brain throbbing as it reassembled

all the pieces, got its house back in order. Her temples ached hard and when she reached up to them, she felt a pair of emerging welts. Bruises. Where she'd struck the rock, maybe.

She had . . . *slipped?*

. . . No, something right at the back of her brain nagged at her, seemed to suggest that this *wasn't* what had happened.

She strained a little harder.

Tried to suck up her surroundings a little more.

That familiar damp smell of rock.

Yes, she was *underground*, that much she could put together in her mind. She had been *caving* . . . that was right, down here in her anorak, her rucksack still hanging from her back like a sag of puss needing cutting off, and her boots still very much tied on tight about her well-socked feet.

The dry thirst in her mouth from doing intense physical activity. When she stirred her tongue, she realised she had a lump of moss jammed in through her lips. It tasted of earth, that dank taste which—thinking about it now—seemed quite preposterous . . . which was to say, *just how had she ever had the inclination to see what moss tasted like?*

Off in the distance she could hear dripping water. And it only served to make her thirst worse. To send her mouth salivating all the more. To send a shudder which seeped in through her skin and rattled her right to the bone.

She could hear footsteps.

Yes, that was right.

Something told her to move, but the spinning of her vision, the darkness which enveloped her, and the ringing in her ears, seemed to strip away any capacity she might've had to do something about the urge.

All the same, she gave it a shot.

Tried to shift herself onto her feet.

When she did that she felt an acute twinge of pain flush through her left shin. It got worse when she attempted to put weight on it and only meant her tumbling back down, onto her bottom, and landing on the solid rock beneath her.

Feeling the wetness from the rivulet that trickled through the cave soaking the seat of her trousers, chilling her to the skin, bringing the hair all over her body to attention.

She felt helpless all of a sudden.

Even despite the torchlight—and the apparent rescue—which awaited her.

But another thing struck her.

Something *odd* about this whole setup.

How the person who shone the torch on her hadn't said so much as a word, hadn't even asked after her, checked to see if she was doing okay, if she was still conscious.

For a second this seemed like an oddity, but she cast it off.

From a lifetime of caving—tracing all the way back to when her father would take her out on *his* weekends, the weekends that her mother, and her Flavour-of-the-Month, didn't claim—she had learned that underground things often weren't as they appeared.

Often.

She *was* dressed in dark clothing after all . . . all black, actually, an extremely poor choice which her father would've no doubt picked her up on if he'd been here—and if he'd still been alive.

That wound felt fresh.

It had a sting to it.

For some reason she couldn't remember *when* her father had died.

Only the fact itself.

She swallowed hard, tried to calm herself, and then she

looked up to where the torch was coming from and said, "Please! Down here!"

She chided herself lightly at that.

At how—even in this, the most perilous of situations—she still managed to hang onto those *manners* the matrons at her boarding school had been so intent on instilling in her.

Sickening in its way.

The way that *that* place still had an effect on her.

Up above her she was aware of scraping . . . some muttered voices, and—of this she was sure—someone uttering, "She's not dead."

All things considered, that was just about the last thing she had time to think about, to think about in any depth, before she heard the unmistakable crumbling of rock above her.

The rumbling roll of rocks falling down.

Landing on her.

Crushing her body beneath their load.

2

SOMETIMES A LONER GETS LONELY.

Even out on the buses.

That's just the way the dice are rolled, how the game is played.

How things work out for a guy.

At least Bradshaw thought as much as he pressed his forehead up against the cool, perspiring glass on the back seat of the Forkesley Regional Express and stared out at the sheets of rain which had seemed to pour down ever since they'd risen up to the foothills.

He looked down to his wide-brimmed hat, which rested in his lap, and then hunched his shoulders, listening to the gentle *crackle* of his leather trench coat rubbing against itself.

His throat felt sore, as it always did when he had a cold coming on.

It wasn't unusual to get colds when you lived on the buses.

When you made a habit of sifting about the most decrepit, the most *broken* of humanity.

But that was just how the dice tumbled.

At least today.

He sucked on the last of his raspberry-flavoured throat sweets —a packet which he'd salvaged from the back pocket of the seat in front of his.

Oh, he'd read the expiration date first, of course, before indulging himself.

And, in any case, he really didn't think there was all that much natural that could kill him considering the amount of chemicals the slick, glistening capsules were packing.

At least not in small doses.

The bus engine whined and whinnied as it climbed the steep incline.

As Bradshaw stared on out through the steamed-up glass, he saw the sign:

Widgsley Caves
Ten Miles

A strange case—but weren't they all in their own way?

He had got a call on the public phone at the bus station earlier this afternoon. That always surprised him. How they always managed to find him. Sometimes he speculated whether someone—*somewhere*—might've manufactured a Find Bradshaw App: the fresh new, must-have kit for the aspiring police officer when the case gets just a little too hot . . . or, more likely, a little too *cold* to handle.

He was the sole passenger on the bus. He hadn't expected anything else.

Just him and the driver.

And, as always, Bradshaw had positioned himself far enough back so as to see of any threat of impending conversation.

That had always been a secret talent of his—being able to keep the rest of humankind at an arm's length.

It took another twenty minutes or so before they pulled up to the right bus stop: the one that Bradshaw had asked after, asked the bus driver to drop him off at.

Where the police were meeting him.

Bradshaw thanked the driver in a muffled voice, stepped off the bus, and then took in his surroundings.

Rolling green hills, thick with bracken, a few twisty, turny trees here and there for variation, and, of course, the great big granite rocks which rose up off the terrain like herds of elephants all migrating off some place.

Or maybe they were all marching on off to the elephant graveyard.

That was one of those concepts which had always fascinated Bradshaw.

Something noble—*dignified*—about an organism which knew its own mortality, its own *place* in the world . . . and which had made peace with it in such a pragmatic way.

And so unlike humankind.

It drove him to despair.

A young policewoman—perhaps in her mid-twenties—greeted him with little more than a stern nod and then led him to the car.

She had short blond hair, and the way that her complexion was fairer about her neck and the cusp of her forehead told Bradshaw that she'd had it cut back recently.

A new life, perhaps?

An appearance could change everything about a person.

As long as that person wanted to change in the first place, that was.

After a whole lot of winding roads, complete with switchbacks, and falls of many—*many*—hundreds of feet, they reached a large dirt open space with an opening leading into the hill they'd just driven up.

This seemed to be the place.

The dirt seemed to act as a car park and though it was only occupied by one other vehicle: an unmarked police car, as Bradshaw swiftly identified it: what with its well-polished, black shell and tinted windows.

A pair of men stood beside it, both dressed in long coats and suits, those hallmarks which Bradshaw had come to identify immediately as detectives.

Here to solve their case.

Bradshaw allowed himself out of the car, and stood up in the fresh countryside air. He could smell long grasses, a hint of dew, and, like always out in the country, that pungent odour of animal dung.

His mouth tasted somewhat devoid of flavour now, in the way that those sweets had of doing to him, of seeming to cause all the saliva to seep out of his tongue—all the moisture to seep out from the insides of his cheeks—and to leave him thirsty as anything.

He drew his leather trench coat tighter about his chest, felt the wind catch the hem of it and blow it up against the backs of his calves.

It was funny how much sound the wind made out in the countryside.

He supposed, with none of those noise-makers like they had in the cities: none of the car engines, or the raised voices, or the marching footsteps along endless pavements, there was only the bare, exposed elements left to make their voice heard.

And that suited him just fine.

The policewoman led him over to the detectives, and he listened to the *crunch* of the tread of his boots against the gravel beneath him.

Neither of the detectives were smiling. Both had that faint-blue hue to their complexions. They both wore pristine white shirts beneath their long coats, and both kept their hands firmly stuffed into their pockets, apparently not considering the possibility of greeting Bradshaw with a handshake.

But that was fine with Bradshaw.

The less human interaction he could get away with, the better, in his opinion.

Bradshaw was still aware of the policewoman hovering at his heels, and he half expected her to be the one to break the silence, the only one with the guts to smash through the ice. However, as it turned out, it *was* one of the detectives—the one with the fresher face, the *less* stubble, who spoke.

"Bradshaw?" he said, his voice an odd combination of expectation and hope.

Bradshaw was used to it.

He nodded in reply.

The two detectives exchanged glances, and then the fresher-faced detective who had spoken nodded to the large opening in the hillside. "Want to take a look while we fill you in on the details?"

Bradshaw nodded again.

They started off in the direction of the opening.

Bradshaw scoped it out in seconds. Saw how it yawned wide as if it proffered the very landscape for their taking. Invited them inside.

How might it have seemed to the victim?

How had she—because he was certain even now, even before having heard the details that it *was* a 'she'—felt about coming here?

Had she been forced?

Hands tied?

Or had it been more innocuous.

His instincts told him it was most likely to be the latter.

But he would keep an open mind for the time being.

The pair of detectives each carried a torch, and Bradshaw was glad for that because he hadn't brought one himself.

As they trod onwards, into the ever-narrowing crevice of the hillside, Bradshaw found himself almost hypnotised by the strange dance of the pair of yellow circles the torches made. He could hear the gentle step of the policewoman on his heels and knew that she was following along behind them at close quarters.

"Pair of guys," the fresher-faced detective said. "That's what we're working with, anyway." He pointed at the dirt floor beneath their feet. "Had some experts come through here to take a look at the footprints, and that's their opinion."

Bradshaw had no comment to make, so he said nothing at all.

Wasted words never served any good.

They only had a habit of strangulating meaning.

The detective gave a long, hard sigh before he spoke again.

"Found her around six in the morning, seems some cavers were passing through." He glanced back over his shoulder, appeared to attempt to meet Bradshaw's eye despite the almost unsurpassable gloom that sprung up all about them. "Dog sniffed her out—always seems to be the way, doesn't it?"

Bradshaw said nothing in reply.

As they trudged onwards, deeper into the cave, Bradshaw was aware of a chill entering the air, and a slight shudder passing about the collar of his jacket.

Bradshaw didn't often shudder.

And the way that his skin formed into tiny pimples put him on edge.

Sent a tingling sensation through his blood.

Just as the cave had got narrower about them, the stone walls of the cave appearing to close in on them from both sides, it now seemed to be widening out.

All traces of daylight appeared to have vanished from the cave.

The torches now shone like a pair of tiny stars—the only thing which illuminated the darkness.

Bradshaw caught the scent of moss in the air, that kind of earthy tang which caught at the back of his mouth, sent another shiver through him, right down to his bones.

He had never liked to be underground.

To feel enclosed with no way out.

That was why he made buses his home.

There was always a way out on a bus . . . come to think of it, the bus itself was a way out.

The detectives parted, one heading to the right, the other to the left. And then they stopped. Bradshaw stood still. Although their torchlight filled the cave it didn't seem to reveal many of the details of the place for quite a few moments.

At first just shadows—vague blurs which represented Bradshaw's arms, his body, and then, gradually, his hands, his fingers.

Bradshaw could hear a *trickle* of water. Apparently coming from down below.

He looked down at his feet, realised he couldn't see the ground beneath him.

That was unnerving.

But he told himself to calm down.

To keep his cool.

Just as he was famous for doing.

Bradshaw crunched his teeth together and then took the few steps it took to go and look between the pair of detectives, over the edge of the cliff where they stood.

In their torchlight, he could make out the flickering reflections coming off the river . . . no, it wasn't a river, it was much smaller—wielded *much* less power . . . more like a *rivulet*.

He could see the forms of several rocks—*boulders*, really—collected all about the shimmering stream. He turned back to the detective who had spoken before though he was fairly sure just what he was going to say next. "Found her down here," he said.

"Crushed beneath all that lot. Took the best part of the morning to get her out."

As Bradshaw peered down there, doing his best to will his eyes to peel back the gloom, to allow him to see the rivulet—and whatever else might be down there.

Just as he leaned a little further forwards, felt that earthy odour of moss become almost overpowering, till he could just about smell the rich—*clean*—flowing water down below, he heard a sob from behind him.

And then a hard, shrill scream.

3

A S ALWAYS SEEMED THE CASE, on the way back in the car, away from the caves, it turned out that Bradshaw hadn't been fed the whole story.

He sat in the front seat of the marked police car—the same one he had arrived in—but this time he sat alongside one of the detectives, the older of the two, the one who hadn't spoken with him back in the caves.

He glanced up at the rear-view mirror, to the unmarked police car which lagged behind them. He could just about make out the two forms sitting in the front seats: the other detective and the policewoman seated beside him.

The policewoman held a whole fistful of scrunched-up tissues and dabbed at her mouth and eyes with them.

As the fresher-faced detective had explained to Bradshaw, the woman they'd found had been the policewoman's stepsister—no blood relation, but Bradshaw could still understand her shock, and sorrow . . . even if he did somewhat call into question just why the detectives had thought it a good idea to bring her along on this particular case.

It was almost as if the detective driving them along, sitting beside him, could read his mind, because he started into an explanation.

"Wouldn't let us say no," he said. "Tried to do our best about it—tell her that she was better off not seeing. But she just wouldn't listen. And . . . well, back at the station, she just seemed to have it all together. Didn't seem like there'd be anything about the thing that'd throw her."

Bradshaw almost thought of putting in his own experience,

of adding just a little bit of wisdom of his own on surrounding people and how they got when those close to them got killed—rather than *died*—but he held back.

He never liked to let on just what he was thinking till he felt he had the complete trust of the person he was with.

And, despite them calling him in to bear on this case—or perhaps *because* of it—he got the feeling that this detective wasn't quite there yet.

Which was to say nothing for Bradshaw himself trusting this detective.

They arrived at the police station in about half an hour, and Bradshaw let himself out of the car and lagged along in the wake of the detectives and distraught policewoman.

When Bradshaw tried to meet the policewoman's eye, she looked away from him, looked to the ground as if ashamed.

He silently wondered if there might be something to that.

If she might've given something away.

There was only one way to tell.

But it would take time.

And so that was just what Bradshaw did as the detectives gave him the tour of the station, leading him through all the evidence they had thus far collected.

Bradshaw found it tricky to mumble in agreement and nod along whenever presented something from the crime scene . . . because his mind was only fixed on one thing.

On getting into a room with the policewoman.

Asking her some questions.

He finally found the right moment when one of the detectives offered him a cup of coffee. He replied to him with a shake of the head, then said, "No, don't drink the stuff."

The fresher-faced detective—the one who'd offered him the

coffee—furrowed his brow just a touch as if this was either some form of insult or some extreme character flaw.

To tell the truth, Bradshaw really didn't care which it was.

4

THE DETECTIVES agreed to allowing Bradshaw into a room with the policewoman, though they were anxious to point out that they had done their best to drag all they could from her.

They claimed she had already given them anything they might be able to use.

It seemed, from the answers she'd given before, that she really hadn't been much in touch with her stepsister . . . or, at least, that was the impression which *she* wished to give.

And so Bradshaw found himself seated behind the grey, steel door of Interrogation Room Two—Interrogation Room One currently resembled something of a greenhouse . . . it did have a rather large window, and so it seemed that someone had taken advantage of that to grow a whole kitchen garden.

Interrogation Room Two consisted of a tiny, boxy window high up in the wall, high enough so as to make anyone trying to peer out—or *in*—impossible, and small enough to make any attempt at escape a folly.

Aside from the window, the only other feature of the room was the rustic wooden table, and the matching chairs, one on each side.

Everything about the room was grey, or seemed that way to Bradshaw . . . and he couldn't shake the feeling that—somehow —they were still down in the cave, as if they still had rocks surrounding them on all sides.

He sat across from the policewoman who had a transparent plastic cup of water before her which she clung to with both her hands.

When Bradshaw looked her over a little closer, he could see that she was—almost imperceptivity—shaking.

He would've said something to put her at ease if he'd been good at that sort of thing . . . but, since he wasn't, he just decided to get right to it.

"Your stepsister," he said. "You weren't friendly, correct?"

The policewoman looked down—down into her cup of water as if she might be reading tea leaves or something—and then she spoke very quietly in reply.

"No," she said, simply.

"When was the last time you saw one another?"

The policewoman gave a slight shrug. Then gave a shake of the head. "Two, maybe three months ago." She glanced up at Bradshaw, made eye contact with him, then added, "I already told the detectives all this."

Bradshaw breathed in deeply, and then out again feeling like he was expunging the smell of moss, from the cave, out of his lungs.

"Tell me more about her boyfriend," Bradshaw said.

This time it was the policewoman that sighed. Her eyes flickered off to the side somewhere—to one of the walls—as if she was consulting with some collaborator.

But there was only one window in the room, and it was high above both their heads.

She shook her head. "It's no good—they already spoke to him. He had a rock-solid alibi."

Bradshaw felt a slight tightness in his chest when he heard her say 'rock-solid' and he saw that the policewoman had registered this oddity in her choice of words too because she swallowed hard —a *dry* swallow despite the glass of water—and then stared back down at the grain of the wooden table where she rested her palms.

"Tell me again," Bradshaw said. "Right from the start."

The policewoman parted her lips and Bradshaw could tell from the way she flared her nostrils, from how her eyes narrowed to a glare, that she was very close to telling him a very flat—and very final—*no*.

She held back though.

And Bradshaw was pretty sure that it was the family bond, however damaged and fragile it had become, being put on display for him to inspect.

"It was so stupid," the policewoman said, with a shake of her head. She flicked a glance at Bradshaw then turned her attention back to her clenched hands. "Like something a pair of school girls get themselves involved in."

Bradshaw crossed his arms over his chest and looked up to the tiny window above their heads. The sunlight shone right through the glass and it stung his eyes to look at it for too long. He breathed in deep, taking in the woody scent of the table and chairs with it.

One side of the policewoman's mouth curled upwards in a wry smile. "She *stole* my boyfriend from me," she said. "*That's* what went on."

Something at the pit of Bradshaw's gut tingled. Perhaps it was a deeper part of himself flagging this up—telling him that this might well be the motive.

His logical mind, though, was the one that finally spoke to him.

Which told him to bide his time before making accusations—before jumping in with both feet when there was no water to break his fall.

"And?" Bradshaw said, instinctively getting the impression that she might be closing herself up.

She gave a shrug. "I didn't like the way he treated her." She glanced up, once more meeting Bradshaw's eye for a fleeting second. "I mean, I didn't like the way he treated me *either*—he really had two sides to him, so often he'd be sweet, and kind, do anything for me . . . he would be . . . *tender*."

Bradshaw turned the pauses in her speech over in his mind, knew that they must be significant. Whether or not they might be feigned, he couldn't quite say.

Her emotion, at least, appeared to be genuine.

But he turned his attention back to the surface level of her story.

"And then," she said, with a slight shake of her head, but still keeping up the same smile from before, "there would be times when he would get drunk and . . . and he'd . . . he'd . . . just become this whole other person—you know what I mean?"

She flashed a glare at Bradshaw as if challenging him to negate her.

But the truth was that Bradshaw knew *exactly* what she meant.

He knew it all too well.

He had experienced it third, second . . . *first*-hand . . .

"Anyway, I told my sister—told *Rachel*—that she should find someone else." She shook her head. "Of course she thought I was just being jealous, like because *I* couldn't have him then *nobody* could . . . but that wasn't the truth, I know that for certain. I just wanted her to get away from him. Just like *I* managed to get away."

Bradshaw breathed deep and long again. Tried to get his thoughts straight on this.

He looked to her again, then said, "You think you can take me for a visit?"

5

THEY ARRIVED outside the home of Adrian Shorth at around three o'clock in the afternoon. On the ride over, the policewoman told him to call her Shelly, and so Bradshaw did.

The home looked just like all the others in the town of Newthrop, which was to say that it was a terraced townhouse, with a quaint little run of concrete steps rising up to the cheap-and-cheerful coloured front door. This one turned out to be a hearty, laser blue. There was a brass letterbox in the middle of said front door. And a pair of broad, double-glazed windows—one upstairs, the other down—looking on out into the street.

Beige, slatted blinds were drawn down over both.

Soggy-bottomed clouds loomed above. A couple of raindrops splattered on the windscreen of the car. The smell of rain filled the air, pressed down over nose and mouth.

Bradshaw drew back from the opened passenger-side window and glanced up to the rear-view mirror, saw the detectives following along behind them. Neither of them made any move to get out of their car. Shelly had told them to hang back and, despite her being a uniform, they seemed fairly pleased to obey.

Bradshaw did realise that—most likely—they were pretty happy to just sit back for a while in the car, maybe listen to a little sports radio.

They thought this thing was over.

That if there was any conclusion to be brought to this rapidly cooling case then it wouldn't be them to bring it.

They might be right.

They might be wrong.

Bradshaw would do his best in any case.

With Shelly alongside, they padded up the concrete steps to the front door. As Bradshaw reached the penultimate step, he heard a *crunch* followed neatly by a *tinkle* of breaking glass beneath the tread of his boot. When he glanced down to see what it was, he saw a light bulb. He'd crushed it into a thousand pieces.

But what had it been doing here, on the steps leading up to the front door?

Before Bradshaw got so much as a second to consider it, he heard the gentle *grind* of hinges. The front door swung back into the house. A man in his late-twenties filled the doorway. He wore a pair of low-slung, black jeans, had days and days of stumble gathered about his cheeks and chin—and making serious inroads down his neck—and an unlit, hand-rolled cigarette dangled from between his lips.

Adrian Shorth, he presumed.

From the state of Adrian's eyelids, the way that they lagged down like some doped-up animal told Bradshaw all he needed to know.

The smell was just a bonus.

This guy was high as all hell.

Perhaps it would've been easier to bear if the only smell coming from Adrian had been his drugs, but, as it was, his body odour—a nasty, sour stench of sweat—clawed at Bradshaw's nostrils, sent chills down his spine.

And he couldn't help but thinking that, if he was to open up a dictionary at the definition of 'scumbag' he'd find this specimen's picture—in black and white—alongside.

It was difficult to believe that Shelly had ever seen *anything* at all in this man.

But then, Bradshaw supposed, he never really had understood women.

Bradshaw drew breath, then looked to Shelly.

As it happened, Shelly was already looking towards Adrian, and Adrian—after giving Bradshaw an exceedingly brief onceover—was looking at her.

Bradshaw noted the change in Adrian's expression, how that hard-nosed look turned a mite softer when he looked over at Shelly.

Then again, Bradshaw had heard all about Shelly and Adrian's past . . . even if he *was* finding it difficult to see himself.

What was that they always said about girls liking 'bad' boys?

"Yeah?" Adrian said, voice gruff, distant, to no one in particular.

Stoned.

Bradshaw gritted his teeth till he tasted enamel, till he could feel the blood pounding in his cheekbones, making inroads into his temples, pumping blood up to his brain.

He thought better that way.

"It's about Rachel," Shelly said.

Adrian snorted hard. He reached up for the doorframe, rested his stubby, brown-stained fingers there. "Dunno what you want about her—been through it all already." He tilted his chin back, glanced over Shelly's head, to the car with the detectives parked up at the curb. "Brought your mates with you, then?"

Shelly flushed a little at this. She averted Adrian's gaze. "Mm hm."

Adrian pouted then brought his focus back to his front step. Back to Bradshaw standing there. "And what the hell you supposed to be?" He gave a smirk. "You look like one of 'em TV psychics, you know them ones that go round haunted houses, stuff like that?"

Bradshaw wasn't quite sure what Adrian meant, but he didn't much care either.

He wanted to get on with this.

Get cracking on the case.

And, the way he saw it, Adrian Shorth was an obstacle to that goal.

"Tell me," Bradshaw said, his eyes clawing their way across Adrian's, "what do you do for a living exactly?"

Adrian smirked a little wider. He reached up, removed the unlit, hand-rolled cigarette from his lips and held it down by his side.

Then he squeezed one of his nostrils shut and then, with the other, and with an extremely hard *blow*, a wad of snot flipped through the air and landed on the front door step just inches from the toe of Bradshaw's boot.

Finally, Adrian said, "'pewters."

Bradshaw didn't see fit to press Adrian for any further answers. In fact, he wanted to get out of this place—out of this *person's* presence—just as fast as he possibly could.

So he got right down to business.

Pleasantries be damned.

"It's believed," Bradshaw began, "that two men were involved in the death of your girlfriend—"

"*Ex*," Adrian broke in.

Bradshaw blinked a couple of times. Found himself derailed just for a moment. "When did the two of you end things?"

Adrian pouted again, shrugged his shoulders, and then looked about an inch above Bradshaw's head into thin air. "'Bout couple of weeks before she died."

"And may I ask why?"

"Jus', stuff and that, yeah?"

Bradshaw couldn't say that he did understand.

And so he pressed Adrian a little harder.

"Would you mind going into a few more details?"

6

ADRIAN SNORTED BACK a whole load of phlegm, and Bradshaw caught the distinct impression that Adrian might well be about to hock it right in his face this time, instead of the comparative politeness of directing it down at the toe of his boot.

Adrian looked as if he was about to throw up his hands, or take a couple of steps back into the house, slam the door shut in their faces, maybe with a few scattered obscenities thrown in for good measure. And perhaps he would've done so if it hadn't been for Shelly catching his eye, somehow managing to wrestle his attention back onto them, back onto the case that lay before them, into uncovering *just what* had transpired to end Rachel's life.

Slowly, Adrian brought his hand-rolled cigarette back up to his mouth, prodded it in through the dry-lipped gap. At the same time as he opened his mouth, Bradshaw caught a good glance at the yellow-brown stained teeth within.

And, just as soon, wished he hadn't seen such a sight.

"Look," Adrian said, the cigarette dangling off his bottom lip, "Shelly, she, you know, got herself wrapped up in some tough shit —with some, I dunno how to put this . . ." for the first time in their acquaintance, Bradshaw noticed a slight cracking to Adrian's tone of voice, a tiny flicker of emotion crossing his eyes . . . a tear or two? . . . "she fell in with a bad crowd, these fellas who came on over here once. Dunno why they came—friends of friends, really. Anyway"—he gave a shrug and a hard sigh which, as far as Bradshaw could make out, was totally subconscious —"she moved out of here a while back, took off with one of them."

Bradshaw removed a notepad and pencil from the pocket of his jacket, handed it over to Adrian, watched as he flapped an arm at Bradshaw as if to say that he didn't have *any* idea about just where these guys might be.

But, with a severe glance from Shelly, he relented.

When he'd finished scribbling away some address in his child-ish, loopy handwriting—half of it capitals mixed in with lower-case letters—he seemed to become just a little paranoid, his attention swiftly switching between Bradshaw and Shelly then back again.

"I, uh, I ain't, you know, gonna . . . gonna get into any trouble about this?"

Bradshaw looked Adrian over once again. Saw that, for all the snot-nosed bravado this guy put on display, he was not much more than a quivering child underneath.

Computers?

If that was what he worked with then surely it could be said that he was afraid of the Big Bad World outside of his front door, and what it might do to him.

Oh, he might've run with the bad kids a while, but now things were coming home to roost.

"Why didn't you say before?" Bradshaw said.

Adrian screwed up his eyes, glared down at the car on the curb—at the two detectives inside of it, apparently talking among themselves, paying the scene outside no attention whatsoever. "Them two," Adrian said, "they brung me in—near enough tortured me, they did. Told me they wanted to know if *I* killed her, if *I* was the one who shoved her off a ledge, let her go flip-flop and land on a bunch of rocks. Bullshit," he said, and then, tears springing up in his eyes he added, "*Bull. Shit*," again for emphasis.

It was then that Bradshaw was pretty sure they were done,

but, just as he turned away from the front door, away from Adrian, glad to be escaping back to the nice, clean-smelling car, Adrian spoke up again.

"And there's the way that they're bad people, yeah? If you get my meaning. Not the sort you wanna mess with, not the sort you wanna have anything to do with . . . especially where the police is involved."

Casually, over his shoulder, Bradshaw said, "Then why're you telling *me*?"

Bradshaw watched the lump bob up, and then down, in Adrian's throat. He was still moist-eyed when he said, "Because I *loved* her," and then, with that, turned on his heel and *did* slam the door behind him.

7

THEY'D DRIVEN about ten minutes away from Adrian Shorth's house when Bradshaw heard the sniffling. At first Shelly took care to keep it under her breath, to keep it so quiet that she was no doubt sure that Bradshaw wouldn't be able to hear a thing.

But Bradshaw had always had a knack of being able to *smell* tears.

There was no mistaking that ripe, salty taste in the air, not to mention the emotional *crackle* that also seemed to pass through it.

When he looked to her in profile, he saw the tears rolling freely down her cheeks.

As she realised the game was up, she relented, taking a hand off the steering wheel to wipe away the tears from her cheek with the flat of her palm. Then she did that thing that *criers* always seemed to do. She broke out in little flashes of smiles—little bursts of nervous laughter as if this was such a *silly-silly* thing to be doing.

Bradshaw could see himself agreeing to *that* sentiment.

"I don't know *why*," Shelly said, "I mean, me and my stepsister, we were never close. Never really lived together. Our parents only met when we were both out of the house. Just a weird thing. A *stranger* really."

Bradshaw glanced out the window at the passing greenery. He could see the clouds all bundling their way up the hills, carting off their rain with them. Hopefully it would brighten up a little this afternoon. A little sun never did anyone any harm.

"And this *thing*, this thing with Adrian"—at this point she flashed Bradshaw a sidelong glance while keeping both hands firmly attached to the wheel—"it was really the first time that either of us have crossed paths, you know, in our *separate* real lives."

Bradshaw checked the rear-view mirror, saw the detectives following close to their tail.

Where they were headed, Bradshaw was certain, they'd need just about all the help they could get.

"I mean, *Adrian*," Shelly continued, "I know he might not *look* much, maybe he looks like a massive loser to you. But you've got to realise that he's gentle, sensitive . . . and, most of the time, a *good* person . . . he owns that house of his, you know, has his own business like he said with computers—put it all together himself."

She let loose a hard sigh. "I fell into that old trap, thought I could *change* him, thought that he'd listen to me . . . and when I realised that he wouldn't, that there was nothing to salvage from the relationship, that was when Rachel popped up, like out of nowhere at all."

Bradshaw reached for his seatbelt, pulled it a little way off his chest. It was a tight fit and seemed intent on squeezing all the air out of him.

When he breathed in now, he could no longer smell the tears.

But that didn't mean they were no longer there.

Sometimes tears stayed inside . . . never quite bubbling to the surface, like subterranean volcanoes.

"Rachel sort of appeared out of nowhere—I wanted to warn her, to tell her what she was getting herself in for, but, maybe, I should've just stayed back, trusted in her judgement, because one thing's sure, and it's that anything coming from me was always fated to get knocked back . . . how could she take it for anything other than jealousy? Some notion of bitterness that I'd left behind something which she'd run in quickly and *taken*?"

To be honest, Bradshaw really had a hard time seeing all the nuances of these soap-opera arrangements, and so he didn't try.

Oh, he trusted they existed.

But that was just about as far as he went.

"And you never saw Adrian again?" Bradshaw said, still staring out the window, not wanting to get an eyeful of a crier again.

"Not till they brought him into the station—till they interrogated him." She drew a shuddering breath which sounded out of place to Bradshaw, since he'd believed that she'd stopped with the waterworks, and then she added, with a wry smile, "Adrian never would've been seen dead in a cave"—she gave Bradshaw a sidelong glance—"if you'll excuse the pun . . . he never was the outdoors type, the murdering type neither."

Bradshaw shuddered to think of the amount of times people had said words to that effect to him . . . so he didn't think about it.

Shelly shook her head again. "Nah, I knew he hadn't done it, and I think, when the detectives got through with him, they knew it too."

Bradshaw glanced down once more at his notebook, at Adrian Shorth's untidy handwriting. At the address where they were headed.

At the names written there.

"And do these names mean anything to you?" Bradshaw said.

Shelly paused a long while. Again she looked away from the road, glanced down at his notepad, and then said, with a shake of the head, "No, nothing at all."

8

THE ADDRESS where Adrian Shorth had sent them turned out to be a warehouse of sorts, pretty much in the middle of nowhere.

Well, that wasn't *quite* accurate, since, as Bradshaw well knew, there was no such thing.

Everyplace had to be *some* place.

It just so happened that the defining features of *this* place was the empty, surrounding hillsides, and a disused railway line running up to the dilapidated building.

Everything about this place screamed to Bradshaw *drug den.*

But he had to hold off for the time being.

Wait till he got some of the facts straight first.

They pulled up and everyone got out.

Bradshaw noticed the pair of detectives feeling for the insides of their jackets, where he instinctively knew any detective worth his salt would be packing something.

Bradshaw looked the warehouse over again, took in the corrugated-iron exterior, the brown stains of rust which seemed to be just as present as the gunmetal grey.

The warehouse was perhaps two, three storeys high, and it looked like a good, firm gust would blow it over at a second's notice.

When Bradshaw breathed in, he got the stench of that unmistakable odour of rusted-up metal on the breeze. That smell that always reminded him of blood. And which sent his heart *tip-tapping* at his tonsils.

He looked to his side, some motion catching the corner of his eye.

He saw that it was Shelly, holding something out to him.

A bottle . . . a bottle of *water*.

He slipped her just about the best smile he could do—which he himself admitted, whenever he had the misfortune of stumbling across a mirror—was a lot more like a *wince*, and then he took a swig from the bottle.

He savoured the fresh gush, that flavourless sensation.

Then he handed the bottle back.

The breeze blew in as they paced closer to the warehouse. He felt its slightly frosty sting up against his cheeks. They crunched along across the dirt ground. He was aware of the two detectives at his heels drawing their guns, holding them down at their sides, and he got a strange sensation of protection—like he wouldn't come to harm here . . . just one of those gut feelings that he had learned to trust over the years.

When they got within ten or so paces from the warehouse, Bradshaw noticed someone peering out from within the opening. Peering out around the corner.

Perhaps he should've held back.

Shouldn't have continued to march forwards.

But he couldn't care less.

He wasn't afraid of death.

When he reached the opening of the warehouse, the person who had been looking out had disappeared. But that didn't mean that he couldn't take in the interior of the warehouse itself.

What he had been expecting—perhaps—was wall-to-wall apparatus to manufacture some sort of drug, something like that, what he found, instead, was far more simple.

Just some hammocks strung about the place from the rafters.

Several burned-out fires.

And odds and sods: large blue plastic barrels containing tinned foods and such.

He glanced back to the detectives, both of them with their

guns drawn, and then he looked to Shelly, as if she might be able to clear up something about this.

But she could only gaze at the scene, open-mouthed.

"Where'd they go?" the fresher-faced detective said as he came up on their heels.

Bradshaw looked about the inside of the warehouse, breathed in the rank smell of body odour, of people who obviously prioritised other things ahead of personal hygiene—and though Bradshaw did live on the buses, that didn't mean he didn't take a shower every day.

"Drugs someplace else?" the fresher-faced detective said.

Bradshaw inclined his head, as if trying to take in the scene from a different angle, or maybe like he was trying to shake something loose from his brain. Whatever it was he was doing, he tuned into the sound of raking, coming from out back of the warehouse.

Without another word to the detectives, or to Shelly, he headed on out to the opening on the other side of the warehouse.

A S BRADSHAW stuck his head out through the opening on the other side, he immediately saw the dozen or so people: men and women, all around their twenties, working at the land: hoes in hand, raking away at the ground, turning the soil.

They all stopped to look at them.

Their clothes were ragged and clodded with mud.

Their faces, too, were dirty.

Bradshaw wondered if there was so much as a fresh-water stream nearby . . . he supposed there had to be if they'd been living out here . . . people needed to drink fresh water to stay alive.

For a long few seconds, Bradshaw's mind went blank.

And then he saw them.

Rachel's killers.

It was nothing more than a simple sidelong glance—a glance which the two men were surely convinced would go unnoticed—and perhaps another less-discerning individual than Bradshaw *would* have let it go . . .

The two of them saw Bradshaw had rumbled them right away, and took off running.

Bradshaw half expected to hear a pair of gunshots from the detectives at his heel, but he knew, at the same time, that as far as the police knew these two men—these two who had *killed* Rachel —were unarmed.

Bradshaw took off running after them, his long, *long* strides eating up the ground beneath the hardy treads of his boots. He thought that maybe some of the other people might resist him, might use their hoes to stop him in his tracks.

But either they had no knowledge of just what was going on here, or they were too stunned to help out their comrades.

Bradshaw followed the men all the way through a heap of bushes, through a bunch of trees, and then to a clearing which saw the men cornered, their only means of escape up a rocky scree which they *were* making an attempt to escape up.

Bradshaw watched on as the men scrabbled up the loose rocks, sending them tumbling as they went. The scree itself was not stable, and Bradshaw watched on as the men gradually slid back along the rocks, not making any progress up to the top.

He had only to wait for the pair of detectives and Shelly to catch up with him to apprehend the two of them and then to cart them off to the car waiting back at the warehouse.

In the meantime, Bradshaw managed to round up the leader of this makeshift commune: an older man in his sixties with a fluffy grey-white beard and sun-soaked skin. He was just about as thin as the hoe which he held up at his side.

He looked surprised when Bradshaw informed him of what the men were suspected of having done, and the man went on to explain, with Shelly standing right at Bradshaw's elbow, how Rachel had been a valuable member of their commune till a little while ago when she had simply disappeared.

It had been the day when she had gone off with the two men they'd apprehended to a cave, to go and bring back some mushroom, or rocks, or some*thing* which Bradshaw instantly forgot the moment the man said it.

What had transpired in the cave, Bradshaw couldn't say.

And he supposed, as he glanced back over his shoulder, to the detectives slamming the men into the back seat of their car, that it really didn't matter.

Not to him.

TIED TO LIFE, UNITED IN DEATH

He had sniffed out the killers.
Brought them to justice.
Now it was justice's job to do the rest.

10

I T TOOK THEM about an hour to get back to the bus station, and for most of the ride over neither Shelly or Bradshaw said a thing.

Truth be told, they really had nothing to talk about.

They were strangers, after all.

Just happened to run into each other through this most grim of chance encounters.

And now they would go their separate ways.

As Bradshaw stepped out of the car, already eyeing the bus heading east—as good a choice of direction as any—he felt a tug at the sleeve of his leather trench coat.

When he looked down, he saw that Shelly had grabbed a hold of him before he could escape. Before he could stick out his arm and board the waiting bus.

"Thank you," she said, this time with no tears in her eyes, not even so much as a wavering to her voice.

She was firm, steady, and Bradshaw could see that she would make a great crime solver one day.

Bradshaw just gave a grunt, nothing more than a guttural sound, and then a nod, gripping the brim of his hat as he did so.

Then she released him.

Let him go on his way.

On towards the next case that needed his help.

The next soul who needed their own truth.

Because, after all, everybody in this world shared one fact.

They were tied to life.

And united in death.

BREAKFAST BEYOND

1

S ITTING HERE, in the restaurant, Mary knew right away this had been a mistake.

As she sat there, feeling pinned into her seat, what with the overpowering *sizzles* and *crackles* which drifted in from the open-plan kitchens, and those smells, the rich scent of basil, and a bunch of other herbs she couldn't have named with a gun to her head . . . she stopped herself.

That was just how she felt now.

Like someone held a gun to her head.

She gave her gum a furious few chews. It had long lost its minty taste and was now more like chewing a piece of mint-flavoured rubber.

She eyed the ladies' toilets, that elegant cursive lettering showing her the way.

She could slip out through the back.

These restaurants always had back alleys, didn't they?

Ways to slip away?

She glanced around. This was an upscale place. Mirrors on every wall. She got that horrible sensation that everyone was watching her. She eyed the maître d' who stood up at the door, awaiting fresh diners, and she knew that he was casting glances in her direction.

The more she thought about it, the more hopeless it seemed.

No, it was too late now.

Or was it?

Why *not* just slip away right now?

She fiddled about in her handbag, with the metal buckle which kept it shut tight.

She peered inside.

There it was.

That little, semi-transparent, brown bottle of pills.

All those white, circular pills pressed up against the plastic inside.

Almost . . . *almost* as if they were *trapped* . . . and she . . . *she* would need to be the one to release them, *nay* that she had the *responsibility* to release them.

"Well, hey there yourself."

Hearing those dulcet tones, the unmistakable low throb in his voice, Mary glanced upwards.

Thomas.

He was here now.

Here with her.

In the restaurant.

Nothing she could *possibly* do about it now . . . not even if she wanted to . . . there would be no escape.

2

TO BRADSHAW, the restaurant really didn't seem to have anything special to it.

One of those white-washed, false—plastic?—looking arch-ways dominated the front door of the place, and acted as a sort of background for the more severe navy-blue tones of the sign, which read: *Giorgio's*.

An Italian restaurant, perhaps?

Bradshaw really couldn't tell, really couldn't have cared.

He never *ate* in restaurants, and when he did it made him feel oddly sick to the stomach, just the knowledge that all those people were watching him, that they were *glaring* at him as he chewed his way through whatever it happened to be: talking slurping, gaping, *heaving* . . .

"Excuse me?"

Bradshaw glanced down, to his left—*way* down to his left, as it happened.

There stood a small, blond policewoman. Her hat slightly out of kilter on her soft, short, blond hair. One thing was for sure, this policewoman right here, she was a good three, or *four*, head and shoulders shorter than Bradshaw was, and Bradshaw was aware that his black trench coat, his ankle-high boots, and the wide-brimmed hat he wore tipped down to cover his eyes, made him out to be somewhat threatening.

He had never set out in his life to *look* threatening.

It was one of those things that'd just *seemed* to happen.

"Can you back up a bit, please?" the policewoman said.

Bradshaw saw where he was standing. Only really seemed to notice properly now. That he stood right up against the yellow, plastic police tape which surrounded the crime scene.

He dutifully backed up a couple of steps, allowed the police-woman to go about her work.

Nobody had called him here—he'd just happened to stop by.

Just *happened* to come across this restaurant with the six police cars pulled up, with forensics in their white paper suits wandering in and out bearing unmarked boxes of *things*.

It didn't seem like they needed his help here.

They looked to be doing just fine.

He should just walk away.

Go for a little stroll through the village.

Hadn't that been the reason he'd come here, by way of a sort of holiday? So that he might stroll along the dew-soaked, cobble-stoned streets, along the crooked alleyways, and past the ancient, wooden-beamed-and-plaster homes?

He had heard that the church here was over a thousand years old.

And so he had been en route to go there.

To go and see whether or not it was worth a visit—if they admitted people for free . . . because, if they didn't, then he would be resigned to walking the circumference, having to be content with seeing those *grey, granite* stones only from the outside.

"Hey!"

Bradshaw looked and saw the same policewoman from before. This time she struck a belligerent posture, one of her hands grasping tight to her hip, as if he was a naughty school-child who was trespassing on some area of the school at lunchtime.

"You can't hang around here," she said.

Bradshaw glanced back at her, gave her a nod, reached up, gripped hold of the brim of his hat, and tipped it to her. Then he wandered on along the road, away from the scene.

Away from whatever it was that had happened at the restaurant.

3

THE CHURCH turned out to charge admission—or, as they put it, a 'donation,' but Bradshaw enjoyed his time there, in the square, all the same.

He only gave up his seat on the finely polished wooden bench, with a plaque dedicated to somebody named 'Begsy,' when an elderly couple descended on him, and he offered his sitting place to them.

The ones needier than himself.

And, with that, he took a final look at the stone church, the weathervane sticking up from its rooftop like an ailing limb ripe for amputation, and he shoved on off along the narrow lane he'd come along, intent on heading back to the bus station.

His route, inevitably, took him right past the restaurant again.

He made a point of walking along the other side of the street so as not to incur the wrath of that policewoman again.

He wasn't out to make *anybody's* life more difficult.

That was one of his maxims.

And he would've strolled onwards, to the bus station, and taken the next bus right out of town, if it hadn't been for somebody calling out to him.

When he turned, looked over there, he saw a man in a suit— a detective?—skitter on out through the doorway of restaurant. He wore a tie which reached right down to his belt buckle. He had a bushy, mud-brown beard which covered most of his face with its thicket.

Still, as he drew closer, Bradshaw could make out that he had bright-blue eyes, and that what remained of his hair—which was little—was lusty and full of life . . . just as bushy as his beard, in fact.

The man was smiling widely, an odd sort of reaction to be brought out from an investigation of a murder scene—because that was surely what the detective was doing here.

The detective thrust his hand at around about Bradshaw's bellybutton, and Bradshaw took it off him.

Gave it a shake.

The man drew back, cocked his head to one side, and pointed at Bradshaw with the twin barrels of his index and middle fingers. "You," he said. "I *recognise* you—I've *heard* about you."

Bradshaw said nothing. He had a bus to catch. It was time for him to move on.

"You, uh," the detective said, glancing about himself, "Wouldn't mind coming on in and taking a look about, would you?" He licked his lips, giving them a layer of moisture so that they gleaned in the first flush of the streetlights which peeled back the twilight. "Could do with a few more ideas . . ."

Bradshaw allowed the words time to tumble out, and then to float on around the air, as if they might mature and take on some other meaning.

When Bradshaw did speak, it was a firm response—but one which, he was certain, was the correct one given the circumstances. "No."

The detective's expression fell in a microsecond. In fact, he settled himself on a fully formed scowl. "What?" he said, the wrinkles now etching themselves deep into his forehead. "*Why?*"

Bradshaw didn't want to get anybody into trouble—it was none of his *business* to get anybody into trouble, because he still recalled the policewoman who'd chided him for hanging about the scene, who had been so intent on him going away.

No, it was better for him to head on to the bus station.

To take the next bus out of town.

He gave the detective his best impression of a smile, and then shucked onwards, heading along the pavement, the bus station already flickering into being in his mind's eye.

He had hardly taken a step before he felt the tug of the detective at the sleeve of his leather trench coat.

He looked back over—*down*—his shoulder at him.

"You *can't* go," the detective said. "Not now that you're *here*."

This detective was beginning to irritate Bradshaw. He would have loved nothing more in that moment than to set foot on a well-heated bus and to meander his way to the backseat where he could prop himself up against the window, tip his hat down over his eyes, and catch some rest before the next thing arrived out of nowhere.

Just like this thing *here* had done.

Bradshaw brought his arm down, attempting to slip through the detective's vicelike grip. And he succeeded. Took another few paces away. The notion of glancing back at the restaurant didn't even occur to him. Not for a second.

When he'd gone about ten paces, the detective said, "Then you leave me no choice."

Bradshaw halted.

"I hereby place you under arrest." He paused dramatically. "For *murder*."

4

A S BRADSHAW examined the interior of the scene, he wondered to himself that one thing was for certain—that the detective certainly knew how to grab attention.

Of course the arrest was a joke, just a *ruse* so that Bradshaw would not be allowed his peace, so that he wouldn't be able to save that policewoman's blushes.

At least she seemed to not be around now.

Presumably headed off home.

To put her feet up.

Lucky girl.

Earlier on, Bradshaw hadn't got a really clear look into the interior of the restaurant. He had only seen the white-marble-topped tables, and the rickety-looking but—on closer inspection —beautifully slick, veneered chairs.

He had expected *blood*, even in a town as quiet as this one.

But, as he stood here, those faint smells of basil, and other herbs floating about, there was no blood at all for him to see.

Not on the floors.

Neither the walls.

Only the marking of where they had found the victim.

Where they had found the *body*.

Bradshaw took in the interior one more time: the candles stuffed into the necks of the emptied bottles of red wine, to the open-plan kitchen which peeked out over the mahogany counter, to the bar area with the upturned, and finely polished, glasses all perched there and ready for serving.

The detective appeared at his elbow. His childish enthusiasm had made a return. And he was clearly *very* pleased with himself at his capture of Bradshaw—of having been able to capture the *uncatchable*.

"Thomas Daugherty," he said. "Forty-six. Time of death approximately twelve hours ago—this morning," he added as if Bradshaw needed clarification.

Bradshaw turned his attention to the other officers buzzing about the scene, and to the vacated restaurant. This was eerie. It *was* eerie. To see a restaurant on a Saturday night totally bereft of activity. No tills being rung. No chinking glasses. No peals of laughter.

Speaking frankly, if those sounds had been present, it would've been Bradshaw's worst nightmare.

But he also understood that some people *did* enjoy that.

Good luck to them.

The detective went on. "Got back the toxicology reports— poison's what they say." He paused and Bradshaw heard the *scratch* of fingernails against loose skin . . . though he didn't want to look, he assumed the detective had been scrabbling away at the back of his neck. "Only problem is," the detective continued, "Not really got any idea about who might've done it . . . in fact, drawn pretty much a complete blank on the thing, if you can believe it."

Bradshaw *could* believe it.

He hadn't garnered his position in police folklore without *believing* it.

Because he was the man who showed up when there was least hope, the one who would offer a fresh breakthrough, who would shine light on whatever the current crisis was . . . the one they'd offered so many paycheques too that he'd become bored with the very notion—the *idea*—that they wished to somehow *tame* him, chain him to a particular place and time, no doubt give him a desk, and perhaps even a tie . . . but that would never happen, not if he could help it.

He liked to help out, but that was where his ambition ended.

"CCTV," the detective said, "didn't pick out anybody really —just that he was dining with this woman . . . we managed to track her down, bring her in, but she didn't really seem to have anything for us so we let her go."

Bradshaw inclined his head in the detective's direction.

The detective, Bradshaw could see, now had a fine layer of sweat glistening across the surface of his skin. Perhaps it was from the high-intensity lights which shone down on them from above. "All the reports," the detective continued, "suggest that the victim was poisoned a *long* while before . . . most likely in the last forty-eight hours, with heavy evidence that, probably, it was closer to the two-days-before mark."

Bradshaw made a low, rumbling sound at the back of his throat.

"Sorry?" the detective said, leaning in. "Didn't catch that."

Bradshaw made no habit of repeating himself, especially when he hadn't said anything at all. And without making a peep this time, he trod onwards, heading along on another circuit of the restaurant, to take in just whatever else needed taking in of the locale.

But he had seen this all—had seen this *all* before.

From every angle.

When he'd gone the whole circumference, and felt the detective almost treading on his heels the entire way around, he stopped, now at the door to the restaurant, and he said, "The woman—where is she?"

The detective whipped out a handkerchief from the pocket of his suit and he did his best to wipe up a good proportion of the sweat which covered his face. He spoke as he continued to dab. "Got her name and address, but *why?*"

"Take me to her."

5

THE CAR RIDE took them the best part of an hour—not that Bradshaw minded.

He welcomed the opportunity to get in a few winks of sleep, to have a chance to allow his brain to rest just for a little while.

He was expending energy on *their* case, after all, so it made sense that he should be allowed some time to rest *his* resources.

Bradshaw woke about ten minutes from the location of the woman's house. When they rolled into the street, he read off the stone-engraved name of the cul-de-sac: *Harvely's Way.*

He eyed the plants growing up out of the rocky walls—from the walls which seemed scabbed with various fungi, and other wilderness afflictions.

The tone of the car engine changed when they rolled into the cul-de-sac, and gravel from beneath them leaped up and pinged off the base of the car.

Three homes occupied Harvely's Way.

All of them identical except for the colours of their walls, and the angle at which they had been pitched.

He blinked away the remainder of his sleep and noticed that the detective was slipping him a sidelong glance. Bradshaw wrestled the detective's glance back. The detective said, "Just weird, that's all—you know, after all I've heard, all them stories, like."

Bradshaw shucked his seatbelt, and stepped out of the car. It seemed that—almost before the soles of his boots touched the ground, he was standing on the front doorstep of the house.

Of Mary Ashkranz's house.

Another few knocks later, and he heard the scrubbing about inside, somebody getting themselves ready to answer the door. When Bradshaw looked to his side, the detective was standing there, hands bunched into fists down at his sides, puffing out his cheeks and smiling in a way which Bradshaw found unnerving.

The woman who answered the door wore a dressing gown. She had deep—*dark*—circles under her eyes while her eyes themselves looked a little pink.

Bradshaw supposed she'd been sleeping just now.

That all this knocking had roused her.

She had sable hair which was sleek and smooth, despite her obviously having just got out of bed. He could see that she had those fragile cheekbones, the ones that reminded him of a bunny rabbit's face.

"Hmm?" she said, her tone of voice floaty, dreamy still.

Bradshaw got right to it. "Why didn't you give him the antidote?" he said.

There was a "*What?*" both from behind him, and from the woman standing in the doorway.

Bradshaw had no time to waste with such rubbish as this, so he breathed in deeply.

And he waited.

The woman's eyes widened. She looked beyond Bradshaw, to the detective standing behind him, and she said, "I thought . . . I thought this was all done with, that . . . that I had nothing else to do with this . . . this *thing?*"

Bradshaw waited for the detective to reply, but nothing was happening. When he glanced back at the man, he saw that he was wide-eyed, and that his lips were slightly parted, in an extremely *gormless* way.

He supposed that he was going to have to do the man's job for him, so he turned back to the woman. To Mary Ashkranz. "Who wanted to poison him?" Bradshaw said, his tone unshakable now—the type of tone he knew, from well-won experience, sent a shiver down people's spines, got them thinking clearly about how they should respond.

"I . . . I . . ." the woman began, but didn't finish.

"Look," Bradshaw said, "we *know* that you had the antidote, so the only reason you had for lugging it about was because you knew that he'd been poisoned and, for whatever reason, you decided that he didn't deserve to be saved."

Bradshaw cocked his head to one side as if seeing the woman from a different angle might make her less dim-witted.

It didn't seem to.

The woman blinked quickly, looked off at the detective, over Bradshaw's shoulder, and then she snapped quickly back onto Bradshaw's eyes, *stared* right into them, and said, "I . . . *can't* talk out here." Her eyes darted about. "They might be watching."

She took a step back, making the silent invitation for them to enter.

Bradshaw, then the detective, did just that.

6

THE SITTING ROOM was like some relic from the fifties —all sun-faded, flower-patterned furniture, with one of those electric heaters that had a poor imitation of a pile of coal moulded onto its exterior. The heater wasn't switched on.

And Bradshaw could feel a chill about the place.

Like an ever-present draught blowing through it.

Though she offered them a choice of the sofa or one of the armchairs to sit down in, Bradshaw took her up on neither. The detective, though, did sit down in one of the armchairs with its back to the window. From where the detective sat—the way the sun streamed in right over his shoulders—it made him out to be a saint of a sort, some kind of *divine* figure.

Though Bradshaw was among the most modest people on planet Earth, even he realised that, here, in this situation, he was much closer to achieving some level of divinity than the detective.

Divine figures often had a job—and they did it well.

And this detective *clearly* didn't do *his* job well.

"Who's watching?" Bradshaw said.

Mary perched on the arm of the sofa for a brief second, then floated on back to her feet once again. She held her hands clutched at her waist like a scolded schoolgirl. Slowly—ever so gradually—her eyes rose up to take Bradshaw in.

"They wanted him dead," she said, her tone flat now. "They wanted Thomas dead."

"And why's that?" the detective said, suddenly chiming in from his armchair. "Need I remind you that, in your statement to us, you didn't bring up any of these suspicions?"

Her eyes snapped onto the detective with such scorn that it

was as if he had just spit on the carpet. "You don't understand what they're *capable* of," she said.

When Mary looked away, Bradshaw caught the detective twirling his finger up at his temple to suggest that the woman might not be in possession of all her faculties.

But Bradshaw preferred not to make up his mind so suddenly.

It blinkered judgement.

Shut your mind off from seeing what was *really* at work.

Behind the scenes.

"These people," she continued, "they'd been after him for such a long time, they—"

"Look here," the detective butted in, "if you're going to tell us anything at all you're going to need to get a little more specific." He paused to draw breath. "*These people* doesn't help us at all." He exchanged a glance with Bradshaw, and Bradshaw was certain that, due to the glance, the detective lightened up a touch when he spoke again. "We need names," the detective continued, "*Faces* . . . we've got to have something to go on, okay?"

Mary glanced to Bradshaw, then back to the detective.

All of a sudden, and apparently without prompting, she broke into tears.

7

O N INSTINCT, Bradshaw took a couple of steps away from Mary.

It wasn't that he was innately cold, or unable to empathise, but there was something about crying which rubbed him up the wrong way—sent a shiver through his gut.

And the way that Mary was crying, those deep, *wrenching* sobs, well, it was just about enough to make him want to puke.

As it turned out, the detective was much better at comforting Mary than Bradshaw ever could have been. Before the first tear had hit the floor, he launched himself from his chair, and latched his arms about her shoulders, drawing her into his chest.

Bradshaw just stood off to the side.

Trying to think things through.

When it seemed like Mary had got a handle on her emotions, Bradshaw stepped in again. "'These people?'" he said.

This time, it was the detective who fired off a look of disapproval in Bradshaw's direction, as if they hadn't come here in the first place to get *his* job done . . . as if Bradshaw hadn't been placed under arrest by this detective—even if it *had* just been a joke—so that he might get this case rolling.

Mary held herself together a little, though her voice was so quiet that Bradshaw had to strain his hearing to catch all the words.

"Investors," she said. "They were *investors*."

Bradshaw studied the way she said it.

The manner in which she said it put him in mind of how an enraptured preacher might intone the name of the devil, or ponder the abstract concept of evil.

That cool, crisp tone which you could hear in a foreign language and still feel the *badness* oozing right off it.

"We," she continued, "*We* were all investors."

"You and Thomas Daugherty?" the detective asked.

She crushed her eyes shut, grasped tight to the lapels of her dressing gown and nodded vigorously.

Now it was like she was channelling some sort of a spirit.

If Bradshaw had ever believed in any of *that*.

She drew in sharp breaths through her nose, apparently getting herself back under control. When she was back with them, she said, "They . . . they wanted him gone—*gone* from the picture."

The detective stood back from Mary only a couple of inches. He no longer held her as if she was a bawling toddler. "What picture?" the detective said, his voice now infinitely softer, as if his main goal was to *tease* out the information.

Mary looked to the detective, and then beyond him, into Bradshaw's eyes.

Bradshaw was certain—just for a second—that he could feel her irises smouldering away right through his brain and to the back of his skull.

"Just some . . . some"—she shook her head, and blared out a laugh which sounded brutal in the stilted air of the sitting room —"*scheme*."

The detective flashed a glance at Bradshaw—Bradshaw flashed it right back at him.

"The antidote," Bradshaw said, head tilted to one side.

"Yes," she said, with a blink, as if awakening from her dreaming only now, "I . . . I *found out* . . . they *knew* that I knew . . . about the *poisoning* . . ."

Her voice trailed away again, but her lips continued to move.

Bradshaw wondered if she wasn't still speaking, just in some register that was below his level of hearing.

"They *warned* me," she continued, "they *told* me that I wasn't to intervene." She snapped back to Bradshaw. "But they were *testing* me—they *handed* me the antidote, told me that if . . . if . . ." her voice spluttered, a couple of tears snaked their way down her cheeks, but she pulled herself together quite swiftly.

"They said that if he *got better*, if the antidote *didn't* kill him that they would know where to come. That they would know that *I'd* done it."

When she spoke the last phrase, her voice raised up into a high-pitched *squeal*.

"And they'd kill *me*."

For a long while, there was stillness in the room. All about them. The words didn't echo—nothing like that. They simply hung in the air till they became drained of all sense and meaning.

At least it was no meaning which *Bradshaw* could divine.

Bradshaw caught the detective as he was opening his mouth, broke in before he could speak. "Thank you for your help," Bradshaw said to the woman, and then turned to leave.

As he strolled on out of the house, towards the front door, he heard the hurried muttering of the detective as he explained something quickly to Mary, before scrabbling up to his own feet and following on at Bradshaw's boot heels.

When he crept up to his ear, he said, "What're you *doing?* This isn't *finished* yet. There's more that she can tell us."

Bradshaw took in the man. Those bright blue eyes that would have looked more at home on a naïve schoolchild, or perhaps on a genetically altered *puppy*. That saggy expression which settled somewhere between shock and confusion.

But which clearly resided in the camp of beleaguerment.

Of being *out* of his depth.

Bradshaw reached out for the door handle. "You have her telephone number?"

"Well," the detective said, glancing back over his shoulder to the sitting room, to where Mary still sat perched on the arm of the sofa, "Of course we do."

"Then we're done here."

And, with that, Bradshaw strode on out of the house, and up the garden path, back towards the detective's car.

8

AS THEY DROVE ONWARDS, Bradshaw had expected a barrage of questioning.

Those little questions where the detective would be *probing* at him—trying to unpick the chain of events that'd just passed right before the tip of his nose.

But he said nothing.

They sat in silence.

Only the purring of the car engine as they returned to the village: to the scene of the crime.

As Bradshaw made a move to get out, he felt the detective grab hold of his forearm.

Bradshaw looked back at him.

Saw the wide-eyed desperation spread across the man's face.

That was something he never enjoyed seeing.

Because, when desperate, men did irrational things.

"We're not done," he said. "The case isn't *shut.*"

Bradshaw looked to the detective's fingers, still clasped to his forearm, digging into the sleeve of his black leather trench coat, then he looked back into the detective's eyes. "You have everything you need now."

He shook his head, apparently struck by disbelief.

Bradshaw restrained the temptation to sigh long and hard, then said, "Check the body. Source the poison—check it alongside the orders, pay particular attention to any start-up organisations, any order that was made by an individual, in particular."

He felt the detective's hold on him loosen just a touch.

Bradshaw was glad to have his arm back, all things considered.

He continued, "*Then*, if you can't find anything *that way* you can get back in touch with Mary . . ." He waited out the beats, expecting the detective to fill him in.

"Ashkranz," the detective said.

That was the thing with cases. Once he'd wrapped one up, he simply forgot the details almost as easily as he clicked his fingers —all those names, the faces, even the murder itself, would be forgotten.

Sometimes he wondered if it was a curse.

Or a gift.

"Yes," Bradshaw said, reaching out for the door handle of the car again, "You get in touch with *her*."

Then, just like that, without the detective saying another word, Bradshaw stepped right out of the car, and back into the cool, late-evening air.

As he stood up beside the still-purring car, he glanced across the town roofs to the setting sun. He watched as its bundling, tangerine form slipped on down, slowly making its way behind the rolling hills which surrounded the village.

Then he cast his glance over to his right.

Back in the direction they'd come.

Just like he'd thought, there was a bus there.

Rumbling into the station.

Ready to take him wherever he wanted to go.

And not before time.

LAMPING THE LUNK

1

CORNELIUS LET THE THIN, seven-foot cardboard box slip from his grip and rest on the curb of the pavement for a moment. It landed with a meaty *crunch*. He could feel himself sweating just about out of every pore. He hadn't expected it to be this hard.

Hadn't expected the damn thing to be so heavy.

He breathed in and out getting that bloody taste of sweat in his mouth, and smelling the odour of his soaped-up, whistle-clean skin leaking out through his salmon-coloured silk shirt.

The shirt he'd bought back when he'd been a Big Deal.

Those sales assistants had told Cornelius, back at that fancy furniture shop, that this 250-litre fridge was too big to be carried between two men, let alone one.

And certainly not for just a pensioner like Cornelius to lug along.

He'd clocked them straight away. He always did.

They'd just seen him for his grey hairs, his flaking scalp, thought about the free bus pass he kept in his brown leather wallet, tucked into the back pocket of his faded lime-green corduroy trousers.

They'd probably also seen his gilt-framed reading glasses peeping out of the breast pocket of his shirt, had seen his wrinkled, pock-marked skin and his frail, wiry chest hair poking through the three undone buttons.

They had no idea who he really was, or who he had *really* been.

Why, ten years back he could easily have beaten those two scummy sales assistants at an arm wrestle at the same time, wrestling one with his left arm and the other with his right.

Hell, he probably could still do it now.

And he certainly could lug a fridge the two hundred or so feet from the shop to his apartment just across the river here.

That wasn't quite beyond him yet.

Didn't need no *delivery* van for that.

Cornelius could just feel the sharp pleat in the legs of his corduroy trousers getting all shaken out. He'd spent all morning getting that pleat good and pressed. That'd be a pain to have to press it in again this afternoon.

But appearance was appearance.

He shifted his weight. Tried to get a better grip on the cardboard box this time with his sweaty palms. He repeated that old mantra of lifting from his knees. That was the key. Who'd taught him that, had he learned that back when he'd worked warehouses?

As Cornelius approached the river, watched it sliding slowly by beneath him, he caught a whiff of the salt water.

And the sewage.

He tautened his muscles even more, bringing the fridge up into his arms a little higher, trying to get better purchase on it. And right as he did so, he caught a glimmer off the surface of the river. He saw his face.

That face.

Stunned momentarily, Cornelius allowed the fridge to slip out from between his fingers. It dropped onto the pavement with a *thunk* but somehow managed to stay upright.

Cornelius stood stock still, staring down at the surface of the river. *Seeing* his face.

The man he had killed.

So long ago.

It *had* been so long ago.

In another life . . .

For what felt like hours, Cornelius remained frozen in time, until he felt a prickling sensation passing up and down his right side before it centred—once and for all—in his chest.

On his heart.

And, staring into those hazel, bewitching eyes, he felt himself slump down to his knees.

Then, a little further in the distance, accompanied by a blood-curdling scream, he felt his head strike the hard curb of the pavement.

Death, he saw now, was just another part of life.

Another time for him to get free.

2

TWENTY-FIVE YEARS EARLIER

THE ICY CHILL off the window sent a shudder across the surface of Bradshaw's skin. He had that grimy—*filthy*—taste in his mouth that he thought could only come from journeys into the City, the *capital,* like this one. He could smell that rubbery, rough scent of the seats. It tickled the back of his throat. It put him on the brink of a half-sneeze.

The rumble of the bus's engine, way up front, down along the aisle, was now so much a part of him that he hardly noticed that it shook his eardrums all over the place.

Bradshaw held his black trench coat jacket tight about his wiry frame. Just as he always travelled, he kept his wide-brimmed hat on his lap. He had his superstitions still. Or maybe it was some small case of manners—taking his hat off indoors—something that his mother, perhaps, had instilled in him.

He peered out through the window as the bus swept into the station. Darkness bled in through the glass. But here it was pushed back by the lime-tinted floodlights which illuminated the bus station. All the other buses were lined up in a neat row, their destinations all marked out in no-nonsense, blocky orange, LED-lit lettering.

Well, he had made it. At last he had made it.

He was back here.

Back in the City.

The bus trundled to a stop at its allotted layby, and then, with a parting shudder—like somebody running their fingertips down a dog's spine—the engine clicked off.

And Bradshaw knew there would be no turning back.

But he had known that all along, really.

Hadn't he?

Bradshaw dragged himself up to his feet, propping himself onto the sure stance offered by his rugged, ankle-high boots. He walked down the aisle with a slight limp. Just like always happened when he sat on buses, his left leg had gone to sleep. It felt like he had pins and needles jabbing into his kneecap.

The police had offered to pick him up at the bus station to the north of the City, but Bradshaw had insisted that he come to this one here. Make the journey—a kind of pilgrimage, really—all the way himself.

Now that he was in the south—the south of the City—it felt almost like he had come home.

And in a way he had.

Stepping off the bus, he felt the chill of the night-time air bite his skin. Bite at his Adam's apple, as the cold always seemed to. One of the only exposed spots on his body. Some days he had thought about investing in a scarf. But, in a way, he enjoyed the sensation. Felt that, somehow, it held him connected to the real world.

He was far enough parted from it in any case.

All that truly remained was to cut the thread.

Once and for all.

But not yet.

He still had work to do.

He trod along the pavement, hearing the gentle *crunch* of the fledgling ice covering the tarmac. He trudged out through the pedestrian exit of the bus station, crossed the road and walked alongside the river.

Even in the darkness, he could make out the stodgy, claylike grey-brown of the water. When he'd been a kid, back here, he remembered staring down into it on his way back from school. And wondering what might lie beneath its surface.

Whether there might be some hidden treasure concealed there.

Or—perhaps—something else.

He shoved his arms into the pockets of his trench coat. He could still feel the nibble of the night wind on his throat. He could remember that feeling from being a kid too. But that had been different. His family never could've afforded something as luxurious as a good scarf . . . well, that was the half-truth, more likely that even if Bradshaw had acquired one, his alcoholic father would've snatched it off him before long.

Just like he had snatched away everything else.

Bradshaw passed by the river quickly, as if it might slop out from between its banks and grab him by the ankles. Tug him down into its salty depths. And out to sea.

Though the police had offered him comprehensive directions, Bradshaw hadn't needed them. He knew the exact spot they meant when they had told him over the phone. Had been able to picture it inside his mind.

He shucked through the side-streets, further away from the river.

The giveaway sign, he supposed, was the blink of blue-and-red lights.

The pair of parked police cars there.

The blue and red deformed the standard, orange streetlights. Lit the facades of the houses up in a carnivalesque rush of colour.

Bradshaw stared hard at the cheery-blue front door of the two-up, two-down terraced house before him. Those familiar —*too-familiar*—seven concrete steps leading up to it.

What, for want of a better term, was *home.*

3

BRADSHAW WANTED TO RUN.

More than anything.

But he had been summoned—they had *called* him here.

So he must stick around for a while.

Answer *their* questions.

Give whatever it was that they wanted from him.

So that they might release him.

And he could be gone . . . once more.

He clutched the metal banister which ran alongside the steps —not because he was afraid of toppling over for lack of balance, but because it was just a habit.

Every day, whenever he got home from school, he would do the same. Clutch on tight to the cool, metal banister that smelled of blood, and drag himself upwards to the door.

To that night's fate.

He would have given almost anything never to return to this place.

But here he was.

He knocked on his own front door, recognising that—just as it had been throughout his childhood—the bell was broken. Its plastic shell crushed. Wires sticking out at odd angles. Like a bug that had been crushed—*crushed* in one of his father's drunken rages.

And never repaired.

Within the house, there was the shuffling of feet, somebody in the front hall, and then—*too soon*—the door swung open.

A silver-haired policewoman, her hat perched at an obtuse angle on her head, peered out at him. Her expression was hard. Not warm at all. And she didn't so much as attempt to raise a smile to him. Then again, why should she? Bradshaw was as much of a stranger here—in *this place*—as she was.

"Yes?" she said.

"I was asked to come," Bradshaw replied.

The policewoman eyed him closely, as if Bradshaw—at any moment—might lurch forwards and attack her. It was only then that Bradshaw recalled that, after striking the door with his fist, he had replaced his hands in the warm pockets of his trench coat. She might think he was concealing a weapon of some kind.

To ease her worry, he gradually slipped his hands out of his pockets—subtly showed them to her as he allowed them to fall down at his sides.

"The son?" she said.

Bradshaw felt a chill creep into his blood at hearing *that* word, but he nodded all the same.

The policewoman eyed him another couple of seconds, no doubt wondering if Bradshaw might be some sort of a wily intruder. One of those nuts who wandered about crime scenes, wanting to know just what was going on. Perhaps even keeping a scrapbook.

But Bradshaw had never made crime a game . . . though it did come naturally to him.

"This way," she said, and then led him off along the creaking floorboards, past the dusty—*grimy*—photographs framed on the wall that repelled Bradshaw's eyes with almost magnetic force.

The air smelled musky, full of whisky, just as Bradshaw remembered. He wondered if all the gins, the vodkas, the rums had seeped into the wood over the years, become an unmoveable part of the house. Perhaps his father would forever live on in this place, even after it was sold on to the next bright-eyed couple, wife pregnant, and never expecting that anything might go wrong with such a perfect urban-family dream.

The policewoman led Bradshaw on through the kitchen, and then to the sitting room.

Though Bradshaw's eyes never left the policewoman's boot heels, he knew exactly where he was, having passed through these rooms thousands—*hundreds of thousands?*—of times.

He didn't *want* to look.

He only wanted facts.

And nothing else.

The policewoman came to a stop in the sitting room and Bradshaw knew that now he had no option but to look up. To look about the place. Or to look to at least where she indicated.

But, when Bradshaw did glance up, he was a little surprised to find a man in a suit standing there—a detective. He had bushy black hair, and he seemed much younger than Bradshaw would've expected. A prodigy perhaps?

"Detective Tawth," the detective said, jutting his hand at Bradshaw's chest almost more quickly than Bradshaw could comprehend.

Bradshaw took his hand off him, gave it a firm shake. "Bradshaw."

The detective dismissed the policewoman with a nod, and she shuffled out of the sitting room, back to patrol the front door, apparently.

When the policewoman's footsteps had disappeared off along the corridor, and silence reigned over the house once more—*that silence, like the calm before a storm*—the detective eyed Bradshaw. "I understand you're the son of Jack?"

Just to hear *his* name . . . it caused Bradshaw's stomach to crunch in on itself. But he was determined not to show anything. Not to this stranger. Bradshaw had made it the habit of his life to keep his past all stuffed down—all nice and buried.

There was little chance he would allow this detective in, allow him to reap through his past memories. Scrounging about like a rodent.

"Yes," Bradshaw finally replied. "His son."

The detective—Detective Tawth—gave a firm nod and then he tilted his head slightly to indicate the room which surrounded them. "We found his body here."

Bradshaw held his gaze firm on a single patch of the roughed-up carpet. Nothing more than a discoloured patch now. He could recall the episode. How he had come home from school one afternoon, lugging his bag over his shoulder. He hadn't known exactly how it had happened, how somehow his father had summoned him to the sitting room. But Bradshaw had fallen for the trick—hook, line and sinker. He had stepped in through the doorway, not noticed his father's trailing leg, and he had tripped right over it. Fallen *smack!* on the carpet. He hadn't thought that anything was the matter until he felt the sting of pain halfway up his leg. And then he had looked to the damp patch of his trousers. The broken glass which jutted out from the material, and his skin. Maybe he'd felt numb, maybe he had suffered enough by then to be able to stand the searing pain, but he had reached down and slid the glass out of his skin. Dropped it back on the carpet, his blood pouring out from the wound. And when Bradshaw had glanced up, his father had said nothing at all. Hadn't even looked at him. His eyes had been back fixed on the TV screen. The multi-coloured light washing over his face.

Bradshaw had hated him then.

Had hated his own father.

A hospital was a lonely place for a ten-year-old boy, but he had done his best to deflect the questions as to where his parents were. When he had returned back home that night, Bradshaw had simply shifted off up to his bedroom. Without a sound.

Just like always.

There was a *snap!* off somewhere in the house.

Both Bradshaw and Detective Tawth spun around to look in the direction.

A couple of moments later, there was a muttered, "Sorry," from the policewoman out in the hallway. "Just tripped over the step."

When Bradshaw glanced up once again, he realised that Detective Tawth was staring hard at him. "The body of the man we found here, we deduced from asking the neighbours that he arrived to stay with your father about six months ago—perhaps as much as a year. Do you know anybody by the name of Storch?"

Bradshaw shook his head. "I was quite distant from my father."

"When was the last time you spoke with him?"

Bradshaw found his mind tracking back to the Last Day. He had always wondered about his emotions then. He must've been elated. Must've been near enough kicking his heels together for joy! And maybe that was so, in his mind—leaving home, finally, at fourteen years old—but he also knew the truth.

That he had felt nothing.

Just numbness.

That same *ripping* numbness he had felt the day his father had tripped him, and he had cut his leg on that broken bottle of booze.

"A long time ago," Bradshaw finally settled on.

Detective Tawth seemed to pick up on Bradshaw's tone effortlessly, and he merely gave a nod. For a few moments, they remained in silence, and then Tawth said, "Listen, I've heard the stories, about all those crimes, out in the countryside. The truth is . . . Mister . . ."

"Just call me Bradshaw."

Tawth continued, "The truth is that I was wondering if you might be able to shine a light on things—on just what's gone on around here."

Bradshaw held himself stock still. So, after all, this *had* been a ruse to tempt him back here . . . back to the *City*. They wanted his expertise—his *gift*, if that was how they wished to describe it.

"Are there any more questions?" Bradshaw said.

Tawth held still, his eyes searching out Bradshaw. Then he gave a shake of his head.

Bradshaw nodded to him and then turned and left the sitting room behind.

Bradshaw had already got himself a good hundred metres towards the bus station, and he could already feel the empty, emotionless night closing in on him, when he heard Detective Tawth's voice echo along behind him.

Perhaps Bradshaw could've continued his walk.

He could've stepped onwards to the bus . . . and back to where he had once been.

But he stopped.

Was that what they called 'unfinished business?'

Bradshaw turned around and looked to the detective, who was now jogging towards him, his cheeks slightly flushed from the cold. When he arrived up beside him, the only sign of his exertion was the thin layer of sweat which clung to his face.

"Your father," the detective said.

Bradshaw wondered if Tawth realised that those words were like daggers in his ears.

The detective continued, "He used to hang around Bleakly Brink, is that right?"

Bradshaw could feel his whole brain swimming. He didn't

want to be here. It felt *unnatural* to be here. Like he was a traveller lost in time . . . somehow come unstuck.

"Just some questions," the detective said. "Just to see if your father is around there." He paused, swallowed hard, and in doing so betrayed to Bradshaw something of a child . . . just like that innocent that Bradshaw had once been. "Please?" the detective said. "You might be able to shine a light on something here."

Off along the street, Bradshaw eyed a black cat sitting on a wall. As it turned its head to inspect him, its reflective eyes caught the streetlight. And for a few seconds it was utterly *blinding*.

Bradshaw looked back to the detective.

Whatever had gone on, Bradshaw was *here* now.

Nothing could change that.

With a slight nod, Bradshaw said, "Just some questions."

4

THOUGH BRADSHAW had never visited Bleakly Brink himself, he had heard tales of it, mostly in hushed-up tones from his mother, as she confided over the phone to some friend or neighbour.

It was where his father went during the day.

Where he sourced his money.

How he kept the food in their mouths.

How he kept Bradshaw and his mother from leaving.

'The Office,' was the only way that Bradshaw's father would describe it.

And that was where Bradshaw was headed now.

To the Office.

Tawth knew just where he was going, and it was a good thing too, because if it hadn't been for him, Bradshaw might've walked past the place a million times without so much as noticing.

It was one of those lounges, one of those which, Bradshaw had been sure, all the Yuppies had demolished and made into blocks of flats in the past couple of decades.

But here was Bleakly Brink, the exception to the assumption.

The façade of the place was a beaten-up burgundy, and the peeling lettering had probably once been gold but was now so faded that it resembled more of a dulled bronze.

And there, sure enough, read the name of the place.

Bleakly Brink

Bradshaw never would've imagined that he would find himself here.

Never would've *wanted* to find himself here.

But—sometimes—there was no other way.

Tawth nodded for Bradshaw to go in first, as if Bradshaw

might know this place better than the detective. As if this place might be in Bradshaw's genes.

Bradshaw saw no reason to hold back now, and he pushed hard against the double-hinged wooden door, and inside.

Years ago, the air of the place had probably been thick with smoke—both from cigarettes and from cigars—now, though, it was only filled with the scent of body odour, and of stuffy cologne. A hint of floor polish hung about the place too, almost like a palate-cleanser of sorts.

The lighting in the place was dim, and faded velvet curtains hung down to cover the tinted windows which looked out into the street. Bradshaw had the feeling that this place would've made the perfect fortress. For whenever these types—whenever his *father's* types—would feel like the wolves were closing in.

There was an old oak bar area with a dozen or so stools drawn up to it. Beer mats clung to the surface of the shining bar counter, and all the bottles of liquor glinted in the little light which penetrated the place.

When Bradshaw glanced around, he was certain the place was empty, and only a guttural, gruff voice proved to him otherwise.

"Help you, gents?"

Bradshaw turned in the direction of the voice. It had come from the corner. He noticed that Tawth, too, had turned to look. Even when Bradshaw had made out the slumped-up figure in the corner of the room, bathed in shadow, he wasn't certain that he could truly unstitch him from the darkness. He took a step forwards. And another.

Now was the time to be brave.

To forget the past.

To *bury* the past.

"I'm Jack Bradshaw's son," Bradshaw said.

The thick wallpaper seemed to absorb the words almost as soon as they had left Bradshaw's lips. Almost as if the surroundings themselves conspired against him.

"That so?" the figure said finally. With a snort, he added, "Jack never did speak about his kid all that much."

Bradshaw didn't answer. He only drew closer to the figure in the shadows, glad to know that Tawth was nearby. "We've come about a body—one which they found in the house." Bradshaw racked his brains for the name. And it came to him. "Storch?" Bradshaw said.

The figure didn't answer right away, and Bradshaw caught the distinct idea that more people had arrived in the room. It was only when Bradshaw glanced over his shoulder, back to the bar area, that he saw that his gut feeling had been correct.

A pair of men stood up at the bar area.

One of them was stick-thin, well-dressed, his clothes drawn tight up against his frame.

The other was podgy, dressed in nothing more substantial than a white string vest.

Bradshaw might've raised a chuckle, if he hadn't been so close to busting open with rage.

Or with tears.

These men . . . he *knew* these men.

He had seen them, from time to time, from between the rails of the staircase as he cowered up on the landing, peering down into the front hall of the house, just wanting all the gravelly voices, all the swearing, to stop.

Neither of the men made a move forwards, but Bradshaw knew that both of them were waiting. That they wanted Bradshaw to be the one to make the first move. To *cause* them to move from their places.

Now able to make out the man's features a little better—his

eyes becoming more accustomed to the dim lighting—Bradshaw caught the man exchanging glances with the two who had just entered. No doubt letting them know, without a doubt, that the man in the suit who accompanied Bradshaw was 'filth' or however it was they referred to police these days.

The man in the shadows turned his attention back onto Bradshaw. "You never been down here before, have you?"

"No," Bradshaw said.

The man tilted his head in such a way that it appeared like a nod, and then he glanced to Tawth. "Guess you're looking for the guy who done in the guy, huh?" He looked back to Bradshaw. "Thinking that it'd be your daddy?"

"We just want some questions out of him."

"Some answers, you mean?" the man said.

"Yeah," Bradshaw replied.

The man sat very still for several moments. He fixed his stare just above Bradshaw's head, looking right into the gloom. He drew in a deep breath which made his shoulders rock backwards and then he gave a hard sigh. "Your daddy," he said, "he hasn't been round here for a while now—that guy . . ." he trailed off as if he didn't know the name.

"Storch," Tawth put in, speaking for the first time.

The man smiled widely. "Storch," he repeated back.

Bradshaw wondered if he'd left that last sentence hanging just so that Tawth would have to speak. Would no longer be the silent hanger-on.

"Storch," the man continued, "he was living at your daddy's place for a while." The man gave a shrug. "How he got himself snuffed, I've got no idea."

Bradshaw didn't believe this man for one second, but, at the same time, he knew that there wasn't much of an option. He wasn't going to drag out that fact with the pair of cronies watching on from the bar area.

"You don't have any idea where we might find my father?" Bradshaw said.

The man parted his lips to speak, and then held back.

It was how people acted when they were on the point of rejecting a request. Bradshaw had seen those giveaway gestures so many times that he could spot them all the way across a crowded room.

But the man wasn't rejecting the request.

The man spoke again. "If I did tell you where I *think* he's located then what would happen next?"

This time Bradshaw realised that the man was addressing Tawth directly.

But Bradshaw decided that it was better for him to answer.

"Just for some questions," Bradshaw said.

"Hmm," the man said, and then glanced over to the two men standing at the bar.

The man slumped himself back up against the bench he sat on and he reached into the inside pocket of his jacket. For a moment, Bradshaw convinced himself that the man was going to draw a gun. But he wasn't. In the end, he withdrew a scrap of paper and a pen. He smoothed out the crumpled paper on the lacquered table top and then scratched something out there in his fierce, loopy handwriting. When he was done, he passed the scrap of paper to Bradshaw who took it from him.

With a nod, the man got to his feet and then shuffled on off across the floor of the bar, and into the darkness of a back room. That left Bradshaw and Tawth alone with the two men at the bar, and Bradshaw could feel the heat of their dual stare on him.

But he tried to put it out of his mind.

Just don't think about it.

Bradshaw led Tawth towards the door of the place, and then out into the street.

They had only got a few steps away before Bradshaw heard a distinct, unmistakable *Psst!* When he turned, he saw one of the cronies who'd stood inside Bleakly Brink at the bar. The one who'd worn the string vest. The sloppy-looking one, the one who, Bradshaw was almost convinced, existed solely to make the snappily-dressed one look better.

He was gesturing at Bradshaw and Tawth, wrinkling up his nose as he did so.

In many ways, he reminded Bradshaw of a rat which has caught a whiff of a cat and is worried that it might find the life snuffed out of it at any moment.

Bradshaw and Tawth headed over to him.

The man worked quickly, scribbling away something on a piece of paper of his own. When he'd finished, he crumpled it up in his fist. His quick eyes slid between Bradshaw and Tawth. "You two want to know where he's really at?"

Bradshaw held still. He felt the crispy cool breeze blowing up the street and he wondered if there might not be a touch of snow in the air later on.

"Gonna cost you," the man said.

Bradshaw glanced to Tawth, who was already digging through his pocket.

"How much?" Tawth said, keeping his voice down.

The man gave his price.

Tawth handed over some notes.

The man passed him the scrap of paper with a nod and then disappeared back inside Bleakly Brink.

Tawth uncrumpled the piece of paper, and then glanced to Bradshaw. "Thanks for your help," he said. "Might've got a little unpleasant in there without you."

Bradshaw touched the brim of his hat. "I'll be seeing you around then."

A slight smile tugged at the corners of Tawth's mouth. "You not heading off on one of those buses of yours?"

Bradshaw kept himself still. Though he would love nothing more than to get himself shot of the City, he knew that, in reality, there was nothing he could do. Something had called him here. He had caught hold of the near unshakeable feeling that no longer could he run away. He had to stick it out. Check out what was going on here.

Even if it hurt.

"Don't fancy coming to see Dad, then?" Tawth said, in a much lighter tone, and one which, Bradshaw was certain, wasn't *intentionally* meant to offend.

But it did offend him.

Any mention at all of his father did.

Bradshaw gave a shake of his head. "You know where to find me if you need me," he said, and then wandered off into the night, headed for the bus station.

Away from all of this.

5

TWENTY-FIVE YEARS LATER

CORNELIUS COULD FEEL them all around him. The constant motion.

An ambulance?

Yes . . . that was where he was now.

Speeding along.

Making it for the hospital.

His chest felt cold and impossibly hot, all at the same time. He could look about him and see the bleary, colourful shadows. The paramedics seeing to him. Trying to keep him alive. Trying to bring him back to life.

But he had been dead for so long.

The only time he had been required to kill, and it had been to take care of his best friend, to toss him into the river with as much indifference as a sack of unwanted kittens.

And though Cornelius had had no questions about the morals of the thing—a snitch was a snitch, after all, no matter how much money they got for the info—he had never quite been able to shake that expression on his face from his mind.

Just like the boss told him to, he had 'lamped the lunk' and got rid.

But, as Cornelius heard the hurried voices all around him, he knew, instinctively, that he was off to join his friend now.

That the two of them would forever reside in death's embrace.

DEAD MAN'S TALE

1

THE LILACS, stuffed carelessly into their white porcelain vase, wilted in the sweltering heat of the church. Their leaves had a brown tinge to them and an odd tangerine-coloured mucus lay on the leaves. And even here, about twenty paces away, the smell was overpowering.

In that tingling, overpowering, warmed-up flowers kind of way.

That tingle started at Jack Shrivner's nostril hair and then quivered on down to his throat, where it got stuck for a moment or two. When he felt the sneeze building up in his cigarette-smoke-ravaged lungs—his lungs that he often thought of as a pair of saggy, sun-bleached red balloons—it felt like they might explode.

He dipped his hand into his pocket, for that ivory-white silk hankie he'd reserved for today—for this wedding—and he slipped it out and brought it up to cover his mouth and nostrils.

Then he sneezed.

He took care of the fallout, sniffling into his hankie and getting most of the moisture out of his nostrils. But that tingle didn't quite go away. And now, to go with that overwhelming lilac stench, he had the taste of mucus in his mouth.

This was going to be a long ceremony.

He had come here alone, just like he always did to family events, ever since his wife, Audrey, had passed away three years ago. This was the first time he'd been in this church since her funeral.

Any church, actually.

Funny that he hadn't thought of it till now.

Her death . . . it had been all his fault. If only he'd thought straighter. Been more organised. If only, if only, if only . . . wasn't life just full of if onlys?

Better to forget the matter.

He would be dead soon, anyway. He would be joining her in the worm pit.

He looked off over to the door. Maybe if he found someone he recognised—even *half* recognised—it might make this makeshift greenhouse a little easier to bear.

That was the theory, anyway.

Blond hair, blue eyes, a crisp, *virginal* white suit.

Looking at him, Jack was sure he was Scandinavian—that he *had* to be Scandinavian.

Jack sniffled a little more, and kept his hankie clenched in his left fist just in case those lilacs saw their way to irritating him again.

This Scandinavian fellow, he had a look about him, a pertness to the way he held his lips, listening with unflinching attention to a man in a suit garbling on at him. But, every so often, Jack noticed the way the Scandinavian would glance away, just for a second.

First he'd look to the woman. His features would soften slightly, that pert mouth suggesting the outline of a smile. And then he'd look to one of the mahogany pews, with the swirls and the polished-up wood. Next to the sturdy slate floor, then back to the gentleman.

Always back to the gentleman.

But that slight squint he maintained seemed to grow more and more pronounced with each sweep of the church, as if, just like Jack, he was about to have some explosive reaction to it.

Perhaps Jack should go over and introduce himself. Offer the man his hankie. Just in case.

Overhead, Jack saw the organ player take her seat, her wispy hair and colourful—slightly baggy—summer dress showing one of her plush, tanned calves. She glanced over her shoulder, and Jack averted his gaze.

Another woman was stepping in through the metal-ribbed, oak church doors now. A lady whose high heels clacked against the slate tiles. She had smooth, creamy skin. And obviously hadn't been on holiday like the organ player had.

He caught her glance as she looked over at a suited man, standing just inside the door. Her eyes never leaving the side of his face as he jabbered on to another suited man, oblivious. And then he watched it play out inevitably, as her heel caught in the space between the tiles and she toppled forwards.

Jack's stomach dipped, but he was glad to see the man she'd been staring at previously reach out and capture her before she hit the hard floor.

Jack turned his attention to the pews.

A large man, in an ill-fitting navy-blue suit with puffs of grey hair about the bare crown of his head, sat forwards in his pew, hands clasped together, head bowed, clearly praying with all his might. Jack saw him mumbling something too. But he had no hope of hearing those words from here.

Jack felt the quiver in the pit of his stomach.

Felt it rise up to his chest.

Cause his chest to tighten.

Too soon.

This had been too soon.

Plain to see now.

Who was he to stand here and act as if everything was normal? As if he had just walked into any old place . . . but this wasn't any old place . . . was it?

And that was when he felt the panic setting in.

His breathing shallowed. His lungs seemed to leak air. And his heart rapped loud in his ears.

He had to get out of here. He had to get out of here right *now*.

As he padded his way along the slate floor, mumbling apologies as he brushed people as he shifted by, he was almost certain that everyone in the entire place was staring at him.

With those *wretched* concerned looks on their faces.

Those slack-jawed half-smiles.

The way they'd fix his eyes and then look away when they felt it safe.

How he just knew that they'd speak about him once they got off back home, how they'd say things like, "Well, Jack's holding up awfully well, isn't he?"

Well, *no!*

Jack is *not* holding up at all well, thank you very much!

In fact he's all bloody torn-up and shredded inside.

. . . But that wasn't what they wanted to hear.

Oh no, they'd like to put off the Spectre of Death, seal him off in a little cupboard, somewhere off in some nook of their house so they didn't have to speak about him till the time came.

Well, for Jack, the time had *already* come!

2

THINGS looked clearer outside. In the sunlight. It was a gentle day.

A light breeze. Blue skies. Twittering birds.

Wonderful day for a wedding, all things considered.

But not any wedding that Jack would be able to attend.

He kept his focus straight ahead as he crunched over the gravel pathway of the church, navigated his way between the cars parked up there. And then he set one foot in front of the other, kept his eyes down so as not to run into anyone he might know—and have to explain why he was headed in the *opposite* direction to the wedding.

He would be back home soon.

Back in his cottage.

In his . . . his *dead* little cottage. Filled with *dead* things. And *dead* memories.

But, he supposed, it was all that he had left.

As he turned the corner, onto the homestretch, headed for his home, he noted a sound in the air. A tootling of some kind.

Trumpet?

Trombone?

Oh, he'd never been all that musical. And, for all he cared, it might've been a violin being bashed over an electric guitar for all the good it did him.

He was about twenty paces or so from his front gate, from his wondrous, picket, white-washed garden gate, when he saw them turn the corner.

A parade, of some kind.

Funny that they'd plan it on the day of a wedding.

But, he supposed, there wasn't a lot of military-level planning that went on in this village—not in Little Inchsham. A clash of events was bound to occur at some time.

As Jack reached his gate, laid his fingertips on the top of the familiar woodcut, he took them in.

A lot of them. All told maybe sixty, or seventy, and still coming.

They filled the whole of the street.

From side to side.

A good thing that there weren't many cars about today.

Or perhaps they had got some kind of permission, succeeded in having the road closed off somewhere. Who knew? Jack was certainly no expert when it came to such things.

He watched them as they streamed past him.

A strange thing happened.

The musical notes. All that blowing and squeaking. All that *drumming*. It seemed to strike a chord with him all of a sudden. And . . . and, well . . . he felt his spirits *lifting* somewhat.

While the music of course didn't take his mind totally off Audrey, of her funeral, it did go some way to relaxing him. So much so that he thought long and hard about turning around.

Of going back to the church.

He *could* do this.

He *had* to do this.

The people streamed past him.

He picked out a couple of familiar faces in the crowd.

Friends. Friends of Audrey. All three of them. Her *best* friends.

The friends that he had always dubbed the Tawdry Trio.

Only in his mind, though, of course.

And every so often when he'd speak to his wife.

She'd never told them about his name for them . . . he was *fairly* certain.

Esmeralda. Hermine. And Georgina.

Why, Jack could recall dozens and dozens of afternoons of bridge in the front room of the cottage. And the gallons of tea they had got through.

He also noticed how the whisky from his drinks cabinet following such meetings always seemed just a shade lighter . . . as if—just *as if*—someone might've made their tea a little Irish, and then tried to dilute the evidence.

Good thing that Jack had always had a terrific nose and palate.

He could taste diluted whisky a mile off.

As the Tawdry Trio passed by, all lavender perfume, exposed, wrinkled cleavage, and fake tan, they—as one—swooped out from the procession and approached him.

And—as one—they beamed their smiles at him.

Not so much as batting an eyelid.

"*Lar*-vley to see you out and about, Jack," Esmeralda said, pouting her lips, and then drawing on his name as if she was sucking on a cigarette.

Jack managed to raise a smile to all of them. "Yes," he said. "It's good to get some fresh air at times."

"And looking so dashing," Hermine said, leaning forwards and seizing hold of the lapel of his suit between finger and thumb.

"I, ah, well, . . ." Jack started, but couldn't finish, since Georgina picked up the slight lapse in conversation.

"You simply *must* take these oorf us," she said, thrusting a box of—what looked like—a box of chocolates.

And, Jack admitted to himself, most likely was.

He received it from Georgina, thanked the Tawdries, and then headed off up his garden path, to the front door of his cottage. Glad to be getting away.

Jack only felt at peace again once he'd got the front door shut —*dead-bolted*—and he was standing on the front-hall mat and breathing his own air again.

Goodness, a wedding could be extremely hard work indeed.

Once he slipped off his stiff—overly-polished—formal shoes, he shifted off to his study. His own hideaway from the world. He guessed that once he got stripped down to his pants, and feeling normal again, he would enjoy the chocolates the Tawdries had brought him a great deal.

Perhaps they would make him feel warmth again.

However fleeting it might be.

3

THE HEAT was blistering considering the fact that Bradshaw had been sat, not half an hour ago, on the back seat of an air-conditioned bus.

Nice squidgy, well-worn cushions.

The gentle *hum* of a sturdy engine.

That dusty, musky *bus* smell.

And nothing but green hills rolling by on all sides.

Now, though, he was sitting in the back seat of a police car, headed up a steep hill, parched as all hell, with the sun shining right on his leather trench coat.

He never thought he'd ever have much cause to feel sympathy for cows. But wearing one's skin now, he could appreciate the ugly face of a warm summer's day.

. . . Well, that would've been true if he hadn't been able to appreciate it before.

Because, as he well knew, ugly things happened every day of the week.

And he guessed he'd seen his fair share of them.

These detectives were good. Both ladies. Smart trouser suits. Not much chat at all

Straight to the point.

He liked that.

They needed him here, and as long as they were willing to accommodate, then he was willing to be here.

He wasn't about to come round stepping on anyone's toes, though, to tell the truth the trouble he usually had with the local constabulary came about from the *penised* detectives.

Gladly there was no such trouble here.

He peered out the window, and looked off down into the valley.

Sheep dotted the fields. All of them with their heads down, munching away at some grass. No cows, though, or none that he could see. He guessed that all the smart cows had long ago taken shelter from the sun under some tree somewhere.

He knew that was what he would've done if he'd been a cow.

The car had a *hum* to its engine too, of course. But nothing on a bus's *hum*.

Really nothing to replace that gentle, almost motherly *hum* of a bus.

He could never quite get himself comfortable in cars.

The truth of it was that he never saw much point to his getting comfy in cars.

He listened as the engine whined its way down the hillside, in that way cars are wont to do, and then slowed its way as they passed by the shingle walls of all these endless, quaint, pale-blue and salmon-pink painted cottages.

Most slatted roofs.

A few thatched.

The cottage they stopped outside had a thatched roof.

Sallow plastered walls.

And a bright-red door.

A *wide-open* bright-red door.

One of the lady detectives cranked off the ignition. She had cropped blond hair and an angular face. A *neat* mouth. She turned in her seat. "Detective Bradshaw, will you be needing anything before we look the place over?"

Bradshaw straightened in his seat. Not too easy seeing as he slipped all over the place with the material they used for these *car* seats. But he managed to get himself straight enough. "Bradshaw," he said. "Just Bradshaw."

The blond lady detective smiled at him.

Bradshaw rubbed his temples. Felt the fizzling throb of nausea eking about his blood. Cars always did this to him. He knew all about *car* sickness.

He unclipped his seatbelt and slid along the back seat, emerged outside the car, standing firm on the curb.

He looked over the house once again, as if he might've missed something, and then stepped through the wide-open, white-washed garden gate.

Just like a lot of these prim little cottages, the garden path was nothing more than a bunch of slabs of concrete all hurled down onto the neatly trimmed front lawn. As he headed on his way, the sickly stench of roses crawled up his nostrils.

Made his sinuses tingle.

If there was one thing that bothered him more . . . or, *as much*, as cars, then it was flowers.

Couldn't stand flowers.

Any kind.

But especially roses.

He glanced back to the car, saw the two female detectives still seated inside. Apparently having some sort of conversation. And then he shoved off over the threshold and into the front hall of the cottage.

DUST LINGERED in the sunrays that beamed in through the windows. The dust floated upwards, and downwards, and all around, never settling. And that, too, got up Bradshaw's nose.

Made him want to sneeze again.

He guessed that this quaint village, Little Inchsham, as he'd read it off the signs on the way up the narrow country roads, wasn't his sort of place.

Give him the back seat of a bus any time.

And a slightly warm, throbbing bus heater.

That was all he needed for paradise.

As he glanced about the hall, he caught sight of the photographs.

Grainy, old-colour photographs. A man. A woman. Man and wife, he supposed.

The photographs showed off the couple in various places.

A sun-kissed beach.

On top of a rocky hill, a sprawling, verdant valley down below.

The two of them on skis, embracing.

Cheeks red with sunburn, and hats pulled down way below their ears. Goggles hiding most of their faces.

A *happy* couple.

Or, at least, that was how it looked to Bradshaw from the outside.

But it couldn't have been too happy. Else he never would've had cause to show up here.

Each of the photographs had a gilded frame about it. Not

polished in a while. And not just a matter of weeks, either, the time since the guy had got snuffed.

No, if Bradshaw had to guess at it, he'd say that the lady had been gone a long while. Either dead. Or divorced. And the dead husband just hadn't seen his way to taking down those photographs.

That, Bradshaw supposed, was understandable.

He moved out of the front hall, taking stock of a mahogany grandfather clock, still clucking away to itself. Its pendulum—just about as *unpolished* as the frames of the photographs—continued to bat from side to side.

He peered round the corner into the kitchen. Saw the sun bleeding in there too. And he caught a sight of the dirty dishes still stacked up on the side. Caught a glint of sunlight off a piece of cutlery lying there too.

Then, off somewhere in the house, Bradshaw heard a light *shuffle*.

He pricked up his ears.

Cardboard on cardboard. He knew that instinctively. Couldn't be anything else.

He glanced in the direction of the sound. Stared hard. Waited.

His pulse tickled his throat.

"Hello?" came a tentative voice off buried somewhere behind the walls.

Bradshaw stepped back, further into the kitchen, and then he glared at the doorway. Waited for someone to walk through it.

"Is there someone there?" came the voice again.

Bradshaw could feel the sweat dampening his lower back. Beneath the weight of his trench coat. And his heart rippled on faster.

Then he remembered the door. The door had been open. But he had assumed that the detectives had opened up the house.

That this was a quiet community, where no one would look at a wide-open front door twice.

Perhaps the detectives had assumed the same.

Assuming never got you anywhere fast.

Bradshaw stood his ground. Stared on. And, not long after, he heard the *pad* of shoes out in the hall. Coming closer to him. Shoe soles on carpet.

And then a man appeared in the doorway.

He was about five-foot-six, maybe -seven, and he wore a beige shirt with a diamond-patterned V-neck jumper. He still had a thick thatch of black hair, though it was surely dyed, going on the wrinkles around the man's eyes.

The way the loose, mole-riddled skin hung off his neck.

The man looked at Bradshaw just like everyone did. Everyone who hadn't seen him before, which was to say just about every soul that walked the planet Earth.

First the man gasped. That was always the first reaction.

And then he brought his arms up to the chest.

The second.

Next, he blinked several times.

As if doing this third reaction would in some way negate the person that stood before them. That *towered* right over them.

But, as far as things had gone so far for Bradshaw, he had never experienced anyone successfully 'magicking' him away with blinking.

He was like a great big lump of coal blocking out the sun.

"I say," the man said, finally regaining his composure, "I didn't hear you knock."

Bradshaw remained silent. His eyes prowling about the man's. Trying to find something. Anything.

"Are you . . . are you quite all right?" he said, taking a step closer. "If you'll pardon the imprudence, I can't say that I recognise you, haven't seen you about the village, in any case."

"How'd you get in?" Bradshaw said, reluctantly shucking his silence.

The man widened his eyes. Parted his lips. "Oh, that, well, yes . . . you see, I was friends—friends with Jack, and, uh, well, the long and short of it is that . . ." he paused a long moment then added, "uh, I have a key to the house." He frowned a touch. "I can't say I recognise you at all, so I'm afraid you'll have to help me out."

Bradshaw breathed a sigh. "I'm here. About Jack."

"Ah hah," the man said, his eyes lolling back in their sockets, "well, if that is the case, then I'll be delighted to help you. Anything I can do for Jack, well, I can't say how wonderful it would be for me to do . . . *something*."

Bradshaw just glowered at him. Waited for something to happen. For this man to shed some sort of light on things.

"Oh!" the man said, with a slight smile. "That's right, haven't even told you my name."

And so he did.

The man's name was Reginald Pipersmouth.

5

R EGINALD led Bradshaw off through the house. He led
him to the room that Reginald referred to as Jack's study,
though, to Bradshaw, it seemed like all there was in the place was
a bare, weak-legged wooden table, washed in that same
mahogany as the grandfather clock.

The air in the room was stifling. The place was a suntrap.
And had been heated up throughout the morning. It made
Bradshaw's throat even more parched. But he could get a drink
later.

First the case.

There were bookshelves too. But the books filed in there were
so covered in dust that he doubted they'd been opened in the last
decade at all. All the lettering on the spines was faded.

He turned back to the study itself.

A chessboard sat on top of the weak-legged mahogany table.

The chessmen all primed.

Ready for play.

The chessmen themselves were all roughly cut. Ones that
would've given him splinters if he'd been inclined to pick them
up. And the condition of the chessmen was strange considering
the prices of property in Little Inchsham must've been astro-
nomical.

Bradshaw's best guess would've been that the chess set had
some sort of sentimental value attached to it.

And so Jack hadn't seen the need to trade up for a weightier,
better-built set.

Bradshaw could appreciate that level of practical thinking.

No unnecessary wastage.

The study had a large window which looked out onto the

garden. Outside he could hear the birds twittering and bees buzzing.

The window looked out onto those roses. Onto the lawn. And, Bradshaw noted, looking upwards, Reginald had opened the tiny window to let the air in.

And all the pollen.

Bradshaw felt himself getting blocked up again.

His nostrils tingling.

But he held it down.

After about ten minutes of conversation, it turned out that Reginald really had almost no information on Jack.

No *useful* information, at the very least.

And so Bradshaw grew impatient as, for what seemed like the hundredth time that morning, Reginald told him some 'hilarious' anecdote surrounding one of their chess matches. Before Reginald could reel into another one, Bradshaw stopped him with a firm, upturned palm. Like a traffic officer bringing a clapped-out hatchback to a halt.

"We know," Bradshaw said.

"Oh, do you?" Reginald said. "You mean, you know just what happened?"

"We know how."

"But not the *who*, is that it?"

Bradshaw grunted.

"Well, I . . . I, uh," Reginald started, and then Bradshaw saw the tears springing up in his eyes. And even though he brought his hands up to cover his face, the tears dribbled their way down his cheeks.

Bradshaw always felt uncomfortable with crying. With *criers*. Never really knew what he was supposed to do. Maybe it came from his childhood. Everything else seemed to. Whenever he'd cried, it had just caused trouble.

So, in the end, he guessed he'd just stopped the habit.

That had made everything much easier.

Much easier to bear.

And so Bradshaw just lurked back from Reginald, waited for him to cry himself out. That was what crying was like. It was like a storm. And you had to wait for it to blow itself out. Then you could start asking sensible questions.

And get sensible answers.

Meanwhile, Bradshaw felt the pollen wreaking havoc with his sinuses again. He sniffled a couple of times, and Reginald caught his eye.

Reginald blinked away the last traces of the tears. He stooped over at the desk and slid open a few of the drawers. "I know that Jack used to keep handkerchiefs handy down here, though I can't say where for the life of me. It's in one of these—ah hah!"

Reginald straightened up, his fist clutching a bunch of clean, white handkerchiefs. He handed one over to Bradshaw, who took it from him.

But Bradshaw didn't blow his nose.

He never blew his nose if he could help it.

He slipped it into the pocket of his trench coat.

"Terrible," Reginald said, gazing out the window, into the garden, and the increasingly blinding sunshine. "I mean—*here*—in Little Inchsham. Who would have thought it? I mean, someone getting shot. It just doesn't happen here, does it? Not at all. Will you, ah, um,"—once again tears sparkled in Reginald's eyes, but this time he held them back—"I mean, will you be able to find the person who's done this?"

"Hmm."

"And, ah, what's the thinking on him? Who did this . . . I mean, if you can say anything about it at all. I can't say I know much about these policing things. Just never looked into it, if you see what I mean? But, what I'm trying to say—what I'm trying to *ask*—is whether you have a vague idea about who it might've been?"

"Professional."

Reginald widened his eyes, and brought his hand up to his lips which were opening wide with apparent shock. "Is that true? My goodness. Whoever would do such a nasty thing?"

Bradshaw grunted.

A silence opened out between them, like a yawning, great hole in the centre of the Earth.

A dry-aired, bottomless valley.

But Bradshaw had no intention of slipping into it.

"Could I," Reginald began, "I mean, if it's no trouble to you, I would like to be involved with your investigations. Perhaps there are things . . . things that I can tell you. Things that you might need to know."

Bradshaw thought this over. If there was one thing that he utterly detested, it was having a whole bunch of people swarming about him, getting all up in his thoughts.

Confusing him.

But this man. He might be useful. Even Bradshaw could see that.

Perhaps he did have something to contribute.

Bradshaw gave him a stern nod.

6

"WONDERFUL, just wonderful!" Reginald said, padding his way across the study, going over to a cabinet. "There is *one* thing you should see. Something that the police just didn't seem all that interested in. But, well, you never know, you might be able to make something of it, though I can't say whether or not it'll be something *really* key to your inve—"

"What is it?" Bradshaw broke in, growing tired of this man that didn't seem to have an off switch for his mouth.

Or perhaps he had lost it.

If Bradshaw had time, maybe he could help him find it.

The cabinet opened with a *creak* of hinges, and the wooden door jerked about as it opened. It looked flimsy to Bradshaw. Not particularly well made.

A little like the chessmen on the little table.

Reginald shuffled about inside. Doing something busy out of sight.

Bradshaw kept his eyes fixed on him. He tried to work him out. That was always important. For him to keep an eye on anyone surrounding a murder case.

Because everyone had secrets.

Reginald rose up onto the tips of his toes. He pawed about around the back of the shelf. And then, with the slide of cardboard against wood, Bradshaw watched Reginald produce a box from within.

He held it clasped in his hands.

A box of chocolates. A dark-purple coloured lid. With all those swirls and twirls, and whatever else box-of-chocolate buyers looked for.

Reginald looked to Bradshaw with an expectancy in his eyes.

His lips apparently on the brink of saying something, but apparently worried about pissing off Bradshaw again.

Perhaps old dogs could be taught new tricks.

But, on this occasion, he did need Reginald to open his mouth.

And, like a faithful geyser, he did.

But not before he'd peeled open the lid to the box of chocolates.

"This," Reginald said, "is what I found in Jack's study, after they'd taken the body away. After they'd . . . they'd said that it was a shooting. That he'd been hit with two bullets."

Once more, the tears appeared in Reginald's eyes, but this time he didn't break down. He carried on. "One in the chest, and one in the . . . the brain."

Bradshaw made a faint mumble of sympathy. Or, at least, Reginald could've interpreted it as sympathy if he'd wanted.

His attention was focussed on the box of chocolates.

A single white note lay across the plastic tray. Well, Bradshaw supposed the note had once been white, since all the chocolates beneath it had long ago melted.

A single, congealed mass now.

Just a block of that dark—*chocolate*—brown.

And the note caked in chocolate.

Bradshaw glanced to Reginald, who'd put his tears away for later again. And then he stooped forwards, snatched the note out of the box between his fingers, and then did his best, holding it up to the light, to read just what was scrawled there.

Though the note was caked with brown gunk, he could just about make it out. The note was written out in blue ink, with a calligraphy nib. And the letters were all swishing designs that told Bradshaw this was someone who had spent serious money on calligraphy lessons.

Someone who had *time* on their hands.

But that meant nothing without the content.

And so he read it over. Hurriedly. Not bothering to read aloud.

He *never* read *anything* aloud.

Not for anyone.

Even himself.

To Dearest Jack,
We hope you enjoy the chocolates!
The Tawdries

That was it. Nothing else added. What now? Another dead-end?

Bradshaw couldn't help but notice that Reginald had sidled up beside him. And that he was glancing over his shoulder. His eyes desperately skittering over the note.

Bradshaw had the premonition that he was going to cry again.

Bradshaw padded his pocket. Withdrew the handkerchief that Reginald had given him earlier. Got ready to offer it to him.

Now, though, looking at Reginald, Bradshaw couldn't see any tears there at all.

Reginald's eyes were just as dry as when they'd met.

And he was squinting hard at the note, as if there was some-thing there that Bradshaw couldn't see. "'The Tawdries,'" Regi-nald said, meeting Bradshaw's eyes. "I . . . I think I know just what that means. I, uh, I remember that once while we were playing chess—"

—Bradshaw prepared himself for another shaggy-dog story, revolving around chess, and gave an internal groan—

"—anyway," Reginald continued, "I remember that just after

Audrey, Jack's wife, had brought us some tea and scones, she'd gone and shoved off again. Gone to answer the telephone. And, though I can't say what she said exactly, I do remember Jack muttering something about 'The Tawdries.'"

Bradshaw gave Reginald one of his best steely glares. And, it seemed, Reginald caught the clue that he should get to the point of the thing.

"And, on the telephone, from the way that Audrey was speaking, well, I just knew who it was. I knew that it was her friends."

Bradshaw slipped a notebook out from his pocket. A pencil too. And got ready to jot this all down.

Reginald gave a little flap of his hand. "Oh, I don't think you'll be needing that. I can take you right *to* them. That's no bother. They all live in the village."

7

A TRIO of phone calls later, and Bradshaw found himself stalking back and forth, up and down the hall. The lady detectives were still sitting in their car. And he had told them to stay just where they were till he called for them. Or, to be more exact, till he depressed the silent Panic button they'd given him.

Sometimes things were much easier when the cops kept their distance.

Because, whatever else Bradshaw was, he certainly *wasn't* a cop.

The Tawdries all arrived at about the same time. And when he heard their tottering heels picking their way over the stone slabs which led up to the front door of the cottage, Bradshaw finally allowed himself into the sitting room.

And he slumped down in an overstuffed—but comfortable—armchair.

The place smelled faintly of cinnamon. And Bradshaw supposed that was an innovation brought into the house when Jack's wife had been alive. He couldn't imagine Jack having thought of such a thing.

The cinnamon, too, got the better of Bradshaw's sinuses. And, after checking the coast was clear, he slipped the handkerchief back out of his pocket and blew his nose hard. Felt much better for it.

The sitting room was much cooler than the study. That was something, at least. And he couldn't smell the roses from the garden.

As he waited, listened to Reginald greeting the women in the front hall, he looked off at the mantelpiece. To the carriage clock.

An heirloom, perhaps. A few polished-up stones. And then, at the very centre, another photograph of Jack and his wife.

This one, though, was of their wedding.

The two of them were all wide grins.

Jack's wife—Audrey, had that been her name?—all dressed in white, her veil floating down over her eyes.

They looked so . . . *happy*.

At that moment, Bradshaw decided to make a break for the kitchen. His parched throat had simply got too much for him. And he *had* to get a glass of water right then.

But, just as he lifted himself up off the sofa something about the wedding photograph struck him. Something he struggled to put his finger on.

What could there possibly be to see in a wedding photograph?

And then it leaped out at him. The familiar face in the photograph.

Back there.

Reginald.

All dressed up in an upturned collar. Brilliant purple lapels that shone in the afternoon sun. And the church in the background. The same one that they'd passed in the car, on their way into the village.

Or, at least, Bradshaw couldn't tell that much difference between one church and the next.

It looked about right.

It wasn't the familiar face, though. That wasn't what unsettled him. Not that at all.

But it was the expression.

The expression on Reginald's face.

He had his eyes scrunched up. His nose almost as upturned as his collar. And there were a series of worry lines set in his forehead.

But he blended in with the rest of the guests almost.

At least, Bradshaw wouldn't have been surprised to learn that he was the only person who had ever noticed Reginald's expression in the photograph. It had only been because he'd recognised his face. The only reason he'd picked him out from the rest of the crowd.

Odd. Extremely odd.

Out in the hall, he heard those distinctive, florid middle-aged —middle-*class*—feminine voices. He thought again about that glass of water, and then decided that he'd just have to get it in a moment or so.

This encounter with The Tawdries shouldn't take too long.

At least, if what he had in mind for the encounter came to pass.

8

BRADSHAW smelled The Tawdries before he saw them. Thick, gut-wrenching, lavender perfume preceded their tottering footsteps. He stayed seated when the first of them stepped into the room. "Well, *hell*-oh there!"

Bradshaw watched the rest of The Tawdries into the room, and then looked back at the first. He pursed his lips and waited.

Just waited.

The Tawdries all stood up straight. He took in their bronzed complexions. Their eyelashes clumped with mascara. And their low-cut tops, showing off wrinkled cleavage.

And then Reginald appeared behind them.

Straight-faced. Glum

So unlike the Tawdries, who were *all* grinning full heartedly.

"What*ever* is this about?" the first Tawdry said.

Bradshaw scanned their faces. He wanted to see if they had any inkling what this might be about. If they'd recognised the detectives sitting out in the car. Outside the house.

Had they put the pieces together?

Their smiles said they hadn't.

But Bradshaw couldn't be too careful.

"I know you hired the hit on Jack Shrivner," Bradshaw said, plainly.

As one, those smiles slid off their lips. Apparently the thick lip gloss they all wore wasn't sticky enough to keep the smiles stuck on.

He glanced between them. Looked for any sign of attack.

Or outrage.

It was Reginald who spoke first, though, but only to say, "I can't say I understand this jump of logic."

And then the first Tawdry, and, apparently, the speaker of the bunch said, "Whatever are you talking about?"

Bradshaw laid his tongue flat in his mouth. He really could do with a glass of water right about now. That'd really hit the spot. Almost there, though.

But not *quite* yet.

Bradshaw stayed quiet. That was always the best option in these circumstances. Let the suspects incriminate themselves. A much straighter proposition.

Sure enough, the first Tawdry just couldn't keep her mouth shut. And she spoke for all of them. Or, at least, that was the theory. "I just cannot comprehend what you are telling us."

Bradshaw studied her features. Saw the slight quiver of the eyelid. The wobble of the lower lip. And he knew that he had hit the nail on the head.

It was just a matter of waiting the thing out.

And then she broke.

The first Tawdry burst forwards. Arms flailing. Those manicured nails clawing through the air.

Bradshaw knew better than to do battle with her.

He jabbed the Panic button in his pocket.

9

I T TOOK approximately forty seconds for the detectives to come bursting in through the front door. And, perhaps, another forty to get all the Tawdries cuffed, and ready to go.

On their way.

As if Bradshaw was their superior, the two female detectives looked to him for permission to take the Tawdries outside.

To shove them into the back of the car and ship them off to the police station.

Bradshaw was reasonably sure, now they knew who had hired the professional hitman, that the police would be able to work things out on their own.

Though he'd learned to understand that they often couldn't see the most obvious things. The things that were right in front of their noses.

And so that was where he came in.

He shook his head at the two detectives. Because he knew that this case wasn't over. Not *quite* yet.

Sure, they'd established the *how* and now the *who*, to a certain degree, but still one of the greatest questions remained.

The *why?*

And Bradshaw was almost certain that he had seen a glimmer of the answer to that *why*, over there on the mantelpiece, in that wedding photograph.

He turned to face up to Reginald, who had remained quite calm throughout this whole process. While the Tawdries had been arrested.

It was as if Reginald anticipated Bradshaw's question, and so immediately took a step back and worked the defensive. "I, uh, I've been thinking about the professional. Actually, I think I might have the answer to that. I might have just the evidence you need to track him down.

"I remember, back in the church, when I arrived to the wedding, and saw that Jack wasn't there, that I noticed this large chap. He was, well, he was wearing a white suit . . . I mean, a *white* suit, at a *wedding*.

"Well, of course, I was thinking about just where Jack might be when I noticed him, and I got the funniest sense . . . I can't say how I would describe it, not much more than this *tingle* down my spine, but I got the impression that we were *both* looking for Jack. And—"

But Bradshaw was holding up his palm again. Waiting for Jack to stop talking. He guessed that he was going to have to spell this out for him. "Look," Bradshaw said, "We don't care. Not about the professional."

"I, uh, I . . . sorry?" Reginald said.

"He'll be gone."

"What?"

If there was one thing that Bradshaw hated more than speaking at all, it was having to repeat himself. Like he was going to have to do now. "*Gone*."

"Oh," Reginald said, and then flashed a glance to the detectives standing there, and then to the Tawdry trio, all of them eyeballing him. And, just like that, Bradshaw saw it clearly, Reginald paled. His face went perhaps whiter than the white suit he had described the professional wearing.

And Bradshaw knew that he had caught another.

Reginald glanced from side to side, and for a moment Bradshaw was certain he was going to run.

Bradshaw rose up off the sofa in anticipation. Ready to block him off. He was certain that he could outrun Reginald two steps to one.

It would be no contest if he tried.

He didn't try.

Reginald bowed his head, like a boy scolded by a school matron. Caught out of his bunk after lights out. *Thoroughly* ashamed of himself.

"I . . . I admit it," Reginald said.

"You admit *what?*" Bradshaw said.

"I . . . I killed Audrey Shrivner. I killed Jack's wife."

All as one, the Tawdry Trio gave a gasp.

Bradshaw looked them over. A slight smile spread his cheeks. Not gloating. Not even satisfied. Just glad that this thing was winding down.

"That's right," Reginald said, in the same doleful voice. "I . . . I, you see, myself and Jack, we played lots of chess"—he raised his eyes to Bradshaw's, as if looking for him to corroborate his story—"and, well, Audrey—bless her soul—she thought that we were spending far too long together. Too much time in Jack's study. 'Cooped up' as she would put it. And . . . and, well . . ."

Bradshaw saw that Reginald was beginning to tear up again. But he had to keep him going. This case . . . these *cases*, were all wrapped up.

Just needed the bow.

". . . One day I just saw her medication, just *saw* it there. Sitting on the kitchen counter. And . . . and it was easy. I just . . . just slipped the bottle into my pocket, left out the door, and that was it.

"When I got home that night I thought of going back, of admitting what I had done . . . but, I . . . I just couldn't."

Bradshaw had no need to press him now for details. The two detectives had heard the evidence. They didn't need to pry any further.

If they did want to then it would be their business.

But, as far as Bradshaw was concerned, his job was done.

He slipped Reginald a parting glare, then turned and headed for the front hall. As he laid his fingers on the latch, felt the weight of the springs, he heard one of the detectives call out to him. The one with the cropped blond hair.

"So, they got the wrong man?" she said. "I mean, they contracted a hired killer to take care of Jack—the husband— because they believed that *he* threw out her medication? . . . But it was his best friend all along?"

Bradshaw looked back over his shoulder. There was nothing else that needed to be said. They could piece everything else together between themselves.

But, all the same, he gave them a solid, unwavering, "Yeah," before he depressed the latch, then wandered off up the street to catch a bus.

A bus that would take him to the nearest regional bus station.

And then, from there . . . who knew?

THE CITY SHE STANDS NAKED

1

EDDY BENT AT THE KNEES, just like he'd been taught to do in his last job at the warehouse by some Health and Safety numpty. He wrapped his arms about the shoe-sized cardboard box which lay on the concrete floor.

Slowly, feeling a layer of perspiration break out on his forehead, a bead of sweat roll down either side of his face, he lugged the cardboard box upward.

Much heavier than he'd thought.

He felt the strain of his efforts pass through his muscles.

Tightening them.

Pushing them to breaking point.

Just what the hell was inside the box?

He only got minimum wage and he wasn't prepared to put his back out for that little pay.

They'd need to give him at least *twice* as much if they expected him to put his body on the line.

About the same amount he'd got paid for playing semi-professional rugby on the weekends all those years ago.

He caught a salty taste of sweat drooling in through his lips. At least it was somewhat more lifelike than that *plasticky* smell which seemed to pervade every nook and cranny of this place.

He managed to stumble his way through the junk in the sound studio garage. He sent little pieces of assorted shit scattering. When he reached the door which led back into the studio itself, he placed the small but incredibly *heavy* load down on a handily placed barstool.

He straightened his back, reached his arms up to the ceiling, trying to work all the kinks out of his muscles. It wouldn't do him any good if he *did* do his back in again. That would mean him lying about at home for months on end. Watching daytime TV. Chewing through box after box of cereal like a cow chewing on cud.

Living off benefits like a disabled.

Till he could get himself back on his feet.

Back into *fighting-fit* shape.

No, he couldn't face that.

He *wouldn't* face that.

Not for the life of him.

As he stood up at the door which led into the music studio, he could hear some kid prattling about with a bass guitar. Playing one of the strings over and over again. He supposed that the kid was tuning up, doing whatever pretentious little rituals they needed to do before strumming their drivel.

Rock 'n' roll was dead, that was for sure.

It'd gone and died in the late seventies.

DO NOT RESUSCITATE

Eddy wondered, sometimes, how the rest of the world couldn't see that.

Refused to see that.

Still, what did it matter to him?

He was well into his fifties now, and he'd be dead sooner rather than later.

Perhaps it was that he no longer fit in this world.

In this *modern* world.

A very likely explanation.

He glanced about the garage.

The fluorescent strip bulb which illuminated the place seemed like it was on its way out. Even standing down here—a full ten, fifteen feet from the roof—he could tell that the whole bulb was stuffed to bursting with dead flies.

He guessed that if the kids who owned this studio caught a

whiff of those flies, they'd have Eddy up there in a jiffy. With a bucket and a pair of gloves. If he was lucky.

Bastards.

. . . How on *Earth* those kids had ended up running a music studio was really beyond him . . .

The rest of the garage was taken up by various cases, all those black shapes that the strip bulb overhead just about illuminated. There were a few bits of metal which reflected the too-bright white tone of the light. This was just a sea of shit . . . it really was.

Why, if Eddy had been younger, if he'd been back in those heady days of youth, he might think of putting this place out of its misery.

Sending it up in flames.

And it was with those thoughts of the smoke in his nostrils— the warm ash rustling against his skin—that he yanked off his fleece. Dumped it down onto some piece of crap or other to expose the white string vest which he wore underneath.

His *wife-beater.*

That phrase always made him smile.

Just thinking about it now made him smile.

Wife. Beater.

Who was it that came up with that shit?

Now standing in only his jeans, rugged, ankle-high boots, and *wife-beater,* he turned his attention back to the box he'd gone and left on the bar stool.

Whatever *was* in that box, it'd better be important.

Else he was likely to bust some heads.

. . . He was just in that sort of mood.

2

BRADSHAW COULD FEEL the cool breath of the city up against his cheek. The winter breeze lightly blowing along the river. Bringing snowflakes.

He could hear the quiet, but unmistakeably clear voice telling him to leave. To get away from here. To catch the next bus out of town.

But he couldn't do that.

Not yet.

He would have to stick around for a while.

Stay here for some time yet.

It was as if he'd sunk down into quicksand, as if the city had managed to lure him in and now its gentle, but insistent, death grip would never let him go.

Never turn him free.

This was everything he had feared.

And *more.*

Bradshaw reached up and adjusted his wide-brimmed black hat, bringing it down a little more snuggly over his long, black, *greasy* hair. It was nights like these—or *early evenings*—that he was glad to have on his leather trench coat. What some might've called a 'wind breaker'.

To keep out the elements.

There was something odd about the air, though.

Not just the feel of snowflakes.

The iciness which clung to the river breeze.

Something *else.*

He breathed in profoundly, trying to get a better handle on his inkling.

Ash.

Smoke.

Fire.

Even the smell of it seemed to breathe warmth into his bones. It put him in mind of barbecues: of grilled sausages, burgers; and all that stuff of memory.

All that stuff behind him.

It was rare that he felt hunger these days.

He just couldn't rustle up an appetite for *anything.*

Perhaps he'd ceased to be human.

Bradshaw realised that, maybe, this smell of smoke was what prevented him from leaving the city. This sense that he needed *to be here* . . . that his most useful, purposeful role in the world right at this moment was *here.*

And so he sniffed the air and headed off in the direction of the scent.

As the ash grew thicker, as he felt the smoke beginning to tickle the inside of his chest—*his lungs*—he quickened his pace.

His sturdy boots clawed their way through the dismal backstreets, the snow already layering down on the frozen pavements. The ungritted roads. But he didn't slip on the ice.

Balance was merely a state of mind.

And he had it in his mind that he wouldn't—*ever*—slip.

Finally, he felt the warmth on the air. Not like it had been before. Not that simple *suggestion* of warmth, but the true, palpable sensation. When he reached up to touch his cheeks, they felt hot.

Like he was coming down with a fever or something.

He trod onward.

Down a side alley.

Then he emerged before the scene of the fire.

3

T HE WINDOWS of the building were all tinted—designed in such a way so that they might be *impossible* to see into.

What caught Bradshaw's attention next, however, was the large, laminated sign which hung up high on the corrugated steel exterior of the building:

X Tracks: Modern Recording for Modern Artists

A music studio?

That was his initial thought, and the one which hounded him from then on.

As he stood before the building, observing the plumes of black smoke pumping out through the roof, he wondered at just what this might mean.

At what this *fire* might mean.

Here he stood, on the pavement outside this music studio, and he could, at the same time, feel the freezing chill of the snowflakes drifting down the collar of his trench coat while the feel of the heat from the building near enough seared his skin.

In the end, it was a voice which snapped him away from these considerations.

"Oi, mate! Give us a hand, yeah?"

Bradshaw tilted his head.

Saw that a large man—in his late forties, or perhaps *fifties*— was dragging a younger, blond man along the ground; from around the back of the music studio.

Bradshaw took in the large man's bald head, and how he only wore a white string vest over his jeans. And how the man had large smudges of ash on both cheeks.

The older man dropped the younger without much cere- mony, to say the least, and then, pointing at Bradshaw, said,

"You keep an eye on him, yeah? Make sure he doesn't turn over?"

And, with that, the man disappeared back into the building.

Back into the music studio.

Bradshaw turned his attention to the younger man, lying crumpled on the cement.

He was propping himself up with his elbow, and his eyes seemed almost to be swirling about their sockets. He was breathing deeply—*in and out*—as if he might be about to have a panic attack.

Bradshaw strolled quickly up to him, crouched down, reached out a steady hand and extended it for the man to grip. With a series of coughs, and—on other days—what might've been a smile, the man reached out and accepted Bradshaw's supporting hand.

Soon enough, the man was back on his two feet.

Standing beside him.

Leaning on him.

Although the ash and smoke was thick on the air—and it almost wrapped itself about Bradshaw's mouth and nostrils—the stink of fire on the young man was overpowering.

Like a mixture of body odour and grime.

But Bradshaw, not exactly a stranger to uncleanliness, chose to overlook this particular detail.

"Are you okay?" Bradshaw said, his voice sounding thick, and gruff, as always.

In fact, it seemed to take the young man back slightly.

Bradshaw saw that the man was wearing a black t-shirt with the X Tracks logo splashed across the front in sparkly silver lettering.

The man wore matching black jeans that had tears at the knee.

Bradshaw supposed the tears had been there before the fire had occurred.

The young man continued to use Bradshaw to steady himself. He was breathing in hard, and then puffing out just as much. When he finally got up enough strength to stand on his own, he managed to put his desires into words. Words which Bradshaw could understand.

"The police," the young man said. "You've gotta call the police."

4

SINCE BRADSHAW hadn't a mobile phone, and, as it turned out, the younger, blond man didn't either—having left it inside the studio—they were forced to move away from the building in search of someone who did.

Bradshaw was reluctant to be seen fleeing such a scene. He knew that it wouldn't look particularly good to any of the nearby businesses to peer out through their windows and see a man of his description—leather trench coat, wide-brimmed hat, and all —fleeing a burning building.

And then there was the question of the other person the young man claimed was still inside the studio. The one which the bald man had gone to save.

They'd got about two, maybe three, streets away from the burning music studio when they ran into somebody with a phone.

A young lady, dressed in a smart trouser suit.

No doubt headed home after work.

Although she clearly wanted to call the fire brigade, the young, blond man—who turned out to be called 'Tony'—was quite insistent that they contact the police first.

Report the fire *second*.

The young lady got through with the call, and then, glancing at her watch, told both Bradshaw and Tony that she needed to be someplace, and tottered off on her high heels.

That left Bradshaw and Tony.

The two of them sitting on a knee-high wall which protected an overgrown garden for—what looked like—a printer's offices.

At least that was what *Inky Pete's Printing & Publishing* put Bradshaw in mind of.

As they waited for the police—and fire brigade—to arrive, Tony turned into Bradshaw. When he spoke, his words were cluttered, all clustered together. And it was obvious that he was still in shock. That might've explained why he couldn't think straight.

Why he'd been so determined that they contact the police *first*.

But, as it turned out, as he spoke, Tony had had his intentions clear right from the start.

"This guy," Tony said, "that bald guy—the one who dragged me out."

Bradshaw turned his mind back to that scene. To the bald guy dragging Tony clear of the burning music studio, then depositing him on the ground before going back to fetch the other.

"Eddy's nuts, yeah?" Tony went on. "Look, around the studio we needed some meathead to go about lugging stuff for us." Tony shook his head and widened his red-veined eyes.

It was clear that he was on edge.

He perched on the brick wall, as if he might be required to break into a sprint at any second.

"He's a flamer, he is," Tony continued. "Looked into his history before hiring him, and he checked out. Just had those past *spent* offenses." He gave a smirk. But never took his eyes off the road ahead, as if the bald man might come barrelling around the corner at any second. "Truth be told, he was the only person who'd do the job—do all the lugging we required—for the pay we were offering. That don't change that he's, you know, a bit"—here Tony made a looping gesture with his index finger at his temple—"*nutso*, if you know what I mean?"

Bradshaw thought that he did, but he couldn't say, without grave doubts, whether or not Tony might be a decent judge of character. From what he had heard so far—from what he had witnessed of Tony—he couldn't quite bring himself to make the same leap.

It could be, of course, that the bald man—that *Eddy*—was in fact guilty of striking the match which'd set the whole studio off burning to the ground. But it could equally be the case that he hadn't. Because, as Bradshaw well knew, the very worst thing an investigator could do while getting their teeth sunk into a crime was to make assumptions.

What was more, it seemed that Tony was one of those people who can only unwind from recent trauma by blabbing their mouth off constantly.

"There was this one time, yeah, when Eddy—when I'd asked him to bring in a bunch of kit, you know, for the drums? Anyway, I was at work, at the soundboard, getting all the levels into place, making sure that the artist I was working with—this *real good* singer-songwriter—had everything just how he liked it."

Tony's eyes bulged slightly. He took a fierce gulp of air.

Bradshaw wondered if he was, maybe, suffering from smoke inhalation.

Tony went on, "Eddy comes in with the kit, lays it all down, and the drummer sets himself up at the back of the sound room. Everything seems like it's going normal, yeah? Like everything's going to plan?"

In the near distance, Bradshaw could hear the first shrill tones of a fire engine's siren.

He knew that they would be on the scene in a matter of minutes.

Something rustled past his cheek, but he didn't stop to check whether it was a piece of ash or a snowflake.

Tony continued, "Didn't think anything of it—we got to recording, playing it all out live, you know, and then, next thing I know, right at the end of the track, I hear this voice of Eddy's behind me. This real, giant, *mad* voice of his, and he goes, 'Aintcha gonna stick a little lead guitar on that?' Well, truth was, I could hardly believe my ears, and couldn't quite believe my eyes, even when I turned my chair around to look at the doorway behind me. Till I saw Eddy standing there—looking like a pissing brick wall."

Here Tony took some time out to cough hard.

He shook his head back and forth several times.

Then he went on.

"Anyway, we'd just got through with recording this really nice little tune, one of those subtle ones, high on melody, and whatever else . . . truth was that I was feeling—you know—just a touch weepy after doing it, and more than a little touchy. So I remember answering him back, saying something like, 'You know, pal, we didn't employ an ape to fling shit.' "

Again, Tony shook his head.

"Way he took it, though, was obviously personal. Maybe he thought he knew something about music—trust me, there's a whole bunch who come on in through them doors of X Tracks and *think* they know something about music. And maybe Tony was no different. Maybe he wasn't no different.

"Anyway, Eddy fixes me with this . . . this *murderer's* glare as if he's gonna split me limb from limb, right? And, well you've seen him, he's a bloody big guy and all, so I got just a little spooked.

"But I did hear, as he was shuffling off down the corridor, back to the little orangutan den in the garage we got for him, he muttered something like, 'burn the place down', under his breath."

Tony stopped suddenly.

Fixed Bradshaw with an unflinching glare.

"Whatcha think of that?"

5

ONCE MORE, as he circled the police cordon, Bradshaw felt the urge—deep within himself—drawing him away from the scene. And, again, he resisted.

It was as if this scene held him in place by some strange magnetic force.

And wouldn't let go.

As night fell, and the bright, white spotlights of the crews illuminated the now-dilapidated music studio—what had once been X Tracks—Bradshaw clung to the shadows, remaining unseen, as was his talent.

He watched the police go about the two men who ran the studio, how they'd both been wrapped up in those tinfoil sheets, the ones designed to keep them from freezing to death out here, in the lightly falling snow.

And then he looked to the bald man—to Eddy—off with his own pair of police officers.

Bradshaw couldn't help but notice that they hadn't yet put the handcuffs on him.

And why should they?

Bradshaw concentrated the most on Tony, who stood alongside the other man he ran the studio with. A man with ginger hair, and a thriving ginger beard.

Bradshaw wondered if he'd got his beard *singed* during the episode.

He hoped not.

It was then that Bradshaw noted a piece of paper—one of many that littered the site—which landed at his feet. He crouched down, looked it over.

His eyes streaming back and forth over the text.

A clue?

. . . He supposed so.

Or perhaps it was just what it looked like: a whole string of numbers.

Numbers which meant, if anything at all, very little to him.

As Bradshaw continued to take in the piece of paper, dabbling his gaze here and there, he heard a slightly nasal— extremely *annoying*—voice up near his elbow.

When he turned, he found himself facing off with a female police officer, about three quarters of his size, and about half as thick. She wore a pair of thick glasses and her frizzy, mousey-brown hair hung down beneath her cap. She held her hands on her waist in a slightly matronly way.

If Bradshaw had had to guess, he would've said that she'd spent most of her childhood in the company of older women.

Where else had she learned such a distinctive gesture?

"What do you think you're doing?" she said, without any preamble.

Bradshaw breathed in the frosty air. He could still taste a touch of ash and smoke carrying on it, but it was nothing like it had been before. When it had been almost impossible to breathe around the burning-down music studio.

"I was just observing," Bradshaw replied, answering as honestly as he could.

"Yeah?" the police officer said. "And you wouldn't mind 'observing' a little way over there, would you?" She motioned a few feet back, in the direction towards the river.

Seeing no reason to resist her wishes, Bradshaw did as she asked, and he watched on as she spooled a handful of police tape to encompass the area where Bradshaw had previously been lurking.

Done, she glanced back at him, and then said, in a tone which almost made him chuckle, "Move along, please."

6

BRADSHAW CERTAINLY did not 'move along, please.'
He had work to do here. He was determined to lend a helping hand.

Whether the police really wanted said helping hand or not.

He kept to the shadows, so far evading the police officer's detection.

In fact, he didn't see her again hanging about the scene.

It was only when he noticed the detectives turning up—in their well-polished black estate car with tinted windows—that he thought to break cover.

As Bradshaw observed the detectives getting out of their car, all suited up: one male, one female; he moved toward them.

He didn't need to say a word.

His *appearance* was all they required to identify him.

If there was one thing Bradshaw was thankful for it was how gossipy police radio seemed to be.

The two detectives shook hands with him.

Bradshaw nodded to both of them, fed them one of his trademarked grunts.

"So," the female detective said, "what've we got?"

Bradshaw noted the female detective's prematurely grey hair . . . at least he believed it to be premature, because it seemed something of an oddity that she might've invested in a facelift and *not* in a quick dye job on her hair.

Bradshaw explained the situation.

What had happened.

How he had been drawn to the scene.

The two detectives listened in to what he had to say for himself.

Once Bradshaw had wrapped up his statement—for want of a *better* word—the male detective thought to ask, "So, you reckon the blond guy—*Tony*—he did it?"

Bradshaw trod along the ground.

As he had been recounting what he had experienced, they had circled the burned-down music studio. And Bradshaw had felt the snow falling harder. Felt it getting down the collar of his leather trench coat. But he enjoyed the sensation. The chill sent a sense of immediacy through him.

Brought him awake just how a coffee might bring around a policeman.

Now they had arrived back around the front of the music studio.

Bradshaw saw that the fire crew was easing down the sign which read: *X Tracks: Modern Recording for Modern Artists*, so it wouldn't come loose and fall on anybody.

"No," Bradshaw said, "I don't think he did."

They stopped walking.

All three of them stood stock still, observing the fire crew for several moments.

Bradshaw wanted to tell them right out.

But he wanted to give them a moment first.

Allow them some time.

"Then," the female detective said, "you think that it *was* Eddy who did it—that he hasn't successfully left his flaming behind him?"

Again, Bradshaw replied in the negative.

Both detectives stared back at him blankly.

Bradshaw knew that he was going to have to fill in the gaps.

Like always.

"I believe both of them were in on it—Tony, and his friend, and that they were hoping to blame the thing on Eddy. What with his history, what Tony was telling me about his character—about his volatile, *fiery* character . . ."

Both detectives furrowed their brows.

Despite his reputation, Bradshaw had learned that it was always like this. That reputation, really, counted for nothing beyond the first handshake. He had to prove himself to those he worked with—those he *helped*—over *and over* again.

He dipped his hand into his coat pocket.

Recovered the piece of paper he'd found lying on the ground.

It was half-burned from the flames.

Still legible, though.

A clue, that was all the detectives needed.

And this might be the start.

He handed the paper over to the detectives.

They both squinted at it, and then the female detective looked up and said, "November—in the red?"

Bradshaw hunched his shoulders in a shrug and, without another word, he turned his back on the officers. He wouldn't have so much as glanced back at them if it hadn't been for the male detective calling out.

"Do you . . . do you know what this is?" he said.

Bradshaw stopped still. He felt the snow stream past his face. It fell much harder now. And he knew that he needed to get somewhere warm. A bus station. That would be perfect.

Somewhere with heating.

Any sort of heating.

Bradshaw turned to regard the two detectives, both of them with their mouths open. "An early Christmas gift," he said, finally, and prepared to walk on.

But he heard, again, the slightly spluttering tone of the male detective.

"But . . . but, what were you doing . . . *here?*"

Bradshaw stared for a long time out into the darkness—into the darkness of the side streets. He wondered if he'd be better off, in the long run, if he just kept on walking. Because these police would speak with other police, as had always happened— as would *continue* to happen.

Sooner or later they would come for him.

They would cuff *him*.

After all, everybody fears the unknown.

But it *was* Christmas, after all. And though Bradshaw had no family of his own, he wasn't wont to ruin the Festive Period for those who enjoyed it. So he turned, and replied, "Sometimes there's just an urge—this uncontrollable desire—*to stay* . . . and it'd take one more foolish than me to ignore that little voice. When the city stands naked, and whispers something in your ear, why—"

Bradshaw was distracted, just for a moment, by a bird flapping off a bare tree branch.

Then he remembered himself.

And he finished, "You ignore that voice at your peril."

With those words tumbling out into the night air, he turned his back on the smouldering music studio—*the pair of detectives*— and he knew that he had done the work which was required of him.

If only he could get out of the city.

If only she would allow him to escape.

Author's Note

Thank you for taking the time to read one of my books. If you would like to hear about my latest releases you can sign up for my newsletter here: www.aviain.com

Thanks for reading!

AV Iain

Trench Coat Country
A Bradshaw Short Story Collection